Bound by Honor

SE Jakes

D1739293

SAMHAIN
PUBLISHING

Samhain Publishing, Ltd.
11821 Mason Montgomery Road, 4B
Cincinnati, OH 45249
www.samhainpublishing.com

Bound by Honor
Copyright © 2012 by SE Jakes
Print ISBN: 978-1-60928-408-4
Digital ISBN: 978-1-60928-373-5

Editing by Jennifer Miller
Cover by Angie Waters

First Samhain Publishing, Ltd. electronic publication: March 2011
First Samhain Publishing, Ltd. print publication: February 2012

Dedication

For you, because you came and asked.

Chapter One

Tanner James had been to hell and back more times than he could count over the course of his twenty-six years and was always pretty sure he'd live to make the trip again. But this time, even as adrenaline raced through his body and every muscle tensed for battle, hell beckoned with a one-way ticket and without a goddamned firefight in sight.

No, that would've been easier, *much* easier than this slow crawl to the door of Crave—a BDSM club with the reputation of being both accessible and safe—the week before Christmas.

He looked up at the dark sign with white lettering at the entrance and thought about turning back and going home.

If he hadn't promised Jesse that he'd do this, that he'd look up Jesse's former boyfriend, he'd be home right now, having just returned from a month-long mission, not about to offer himself up like some bondage sacrifice.

This wasn't his scene. Not really. He was all about rough sex, was bisexual with a definite preference to men for as long as he could remember, used to having to *don't ask, don't tell*, thanks to his military career—but this? Having to go in and greet the owner with a message from his dead lover? Well, that was fucking weird and could get him thrown out on his ass.

Jesus Christ, this was going to suck.

The man checking patrons who entered was dressed in

bright, loud colors. Tight black leather pants. Guyliner. And he flirted in an over-the-top manner with anyone he deemed hot enough.

Tanner knew he'd be the subject of the man's flirtation. Although he'd shrugged it off his entire life, the looks and stares and come-ons he'd been on the receiving end of forever told him he was handsome.

He was more interested in being the best Army Ranger he could, spent most days knee-deep in jungle crap with paint on his face and men who only cared that he could shoot an M-14 with dizzying accuracy.

"Hey."

"Hello, gorgeous. Please tell me you're alone." The man peeked behind Tanner, saw no one and clapped his hands. "Alone. There is a God."

"I'm looking for Damon Price."

"I'll bet you are," the man said with a shake of his head. "Shame, really, that they all want what they can't have."

"I just need to talk to him."

The man erupted into peals of girlish laughter and Tanner rolled his eyes. He'd never been into queens and this was why. If he was going to fuck a man, he was going to fuck a man. "Tell him I've got a message from Jesse."

The man stopped, nearly choked, but before he could answer, he was elbowed out of the way by a much taller blond man—ruggedly handsome although unsmiling, and Tanner wondered if he was face to face with Damon himself.

But rather than introduce himself, he asked, "What did you say about Jesse?"

"You heard me," Tanner bit out.

The man nodded slowly. "I heard you. I just don't know

how Damon's going to feel about this." He paused. "Are you sure you want to go there?"

Tanner reacted before he could stop himself. "Why the *fuck* would you care where I want to go?"

The man raised a brow and held up a finger, indicating for Tanner to wait a minute, before disappearing down a back hallway.

Last chance to head for the hills. And despite the ease with which he could do so, Tanner remained rooted in place.

He couldn't see very far into the club at all from where he stood—it was designed purposely to let the incoming patrons hear the familiar sounds of sex occasionally rising over the music. The smell of sex was also unmistakable, partially hidden and mixed with whiskey and smoke. It was meant to beckon, to lead men astray...and Tanner didn't bother to hide his hard-on.

A few minutes later, Tanner was being led by the blond man who introduced himself as LC back to a private office with a big *Do Not Disturb* sign on the door.

No doubt, *this* counted as disturbing Damon, but it had been eating away at Tanner for a year now. He had to rid himself of this burden, do what Jesse asked and then go home and pretend none of it ever happened.

Before going in, he glanced at his watch. Just after midnight. Exactly the way Jesse had wanted it.

A hard growl of a voice called, "Come in."

LC stared at him, and Tanner, in turn, stared at the floor for a long moment. And then he opened the door and realized he'd been anything but prepared for Damon Price. Tanner was big and broad and strong, stood six foot three and turned heads wherever he went. But Damon—he was well over six foot five, with jet black hair and chiseled features. He stood, hands at his sides in a deceptively casual stance, dressed in full black

11

leather and looking like a fucking badass.

Tanner nearly hyperventilated, because Jesse hadn't mentioned this part.

"He's my boyfriend and he owns a club," was all Jesse said. *"He's strong—reminds me of you. He's a Dom."*

"I'm not a Dom."

"No. But you could probably use one. It would be the only kind of man who could handle you."

Jesse had closed his eyes then before Tanner could tell him he had no interest in being anyone's bottom boy. Because Jesse had been talking to him about boyfriends and Doms when he'd been dying, slowly and painfully in the middle of a jungle in South America where he and his Ranger team had been on a mission, and Tanner had been fucking helpless to stop it.

Fuck.

He shoved his hands in his pockets so Damon wouldn't see the fists he couldn't uncurl and hoped the pain didn't show in his eyes.

This was supposed to bring closure—to both Damon and Tanner. There was no way to break a promise to a dead man.

Damon studied him for a few minutes. Tanner wasn't the type to squirm and he wasn't about to start now. Finally, the man said, "I hear you have a message from Jesse. And I swear to Christ, if you're fucking with me, I'll put your head through the wall."

Tanner snorted in spite of himself. "Okay, sure. I'd like to see you try."

Damon pushed away from the desk and stood toe-to-toe with him. "Talk."

Talk. Yeah, like it was that easy. "Jesse told me to come here—to ask for you. To tell you that..." Fuck. He shifted, aware that the proximity of Damon was freaking him out. If he hadn't been Jesse's, Tanner might've made a move without a second thought.

As if he knew what he was thinking, Damon arched an eyebrow at him, his lip curled into a half sneer.

Fuck it all. "I'm supposed to tell you to have a session with me. Jesse wanted it that way."

"A session?" Damon repeated.

"Yeah. I'm supposed to let you Dom me. It was Jesse's dying wish."

Damon paled, took a step back from Tanner, and then another. "Is this a sick joke?"

"Do I look like I'm joking?"

"You little fuck." Damon had Tanner's shirt bunched in his fists, was slamming him against the office wall hard. "You sick bastard. You think you can ingratiate yourself to me by using Jesse?"

Tanner ground his teeth together hard and tamped back his anger. He'd known Damon wouldn't take this well. If Tanner had been in the same position, he doubted he would either. "He asked me to wait a year before I came here. He died after midnight."

"How do you know that?" Damon demanded. "Even I don't know that."

No, he wouldn't. The mission was deemed classified—and Jesse's time of death a closely guarded secret. "I was with him when he died."

Damon let out a long, hissing breath and let go of Tanner's shirt.

"I'm sorry—I didn't know how else to tell you. Jesse made me promise—"

"Stop saying his name," Damon growled hoarsely.

"He made me promise I'd wait the year. Said you wouldn't be ready before that. That you'd need to be dragged back into the land of the living, kicking and screaming. He said to tell you...to use the skull-and-crossbones collar with the broken latch." He spoke fast, stopped to catch his breath at the end. Gauged Damon's reaction.

The man hadn't moved a muscle during Tanner's speech. Simply stared, and Tanner tensed more, wondering if he was going to have to fight tonight.

Fighting and fucking were definitely two of his favorite things to do, sometimes all in the same night—or hour—or hell, the same time, but he had a feeling that he'd be pushing his luck taking on this guy.

He was in way over his head. And he couldn't remember the last time—if ever—he'd felt that way.

Damon's features relaxed slightly. He sat back on the top of the desk, folded his arms and stared Tanner up and down. A hard, assessing stare that was enough to make Tanner hard with desire and anticipation.

He wasn't sure why the sudden thought of Damon taking him got him hot, but that was short-lived, because he saw the tension in Damon's stance, the pain in his eyes. Tanner wanted to apologize, but he wasn't sure what for. Wanted to tell Damon that he was scared to fucking death that the Domming would actually happen—and also scared that it wouldn't.

He was so fucked up he could barely see straight.

Damon finally spoke. "I wouldn't touch you. You're not man enough to handle me."

Jesse's words echoed in Tanner's ear. *It would be the only kind of man who could handle you.*

Tanner hadn't been able to handle a relationship—or being touched, really, since what happened to Jesse last year. And so he nodded and he said, "You're right about that. This was a mistake."

The failure hanging on him heavily, he pushed out the door, went through the club and headed for the parking lot.

Jesse.

Damon had mourned over that man, cried over him, beat his fists against the wall, up until three months earlier. Things had eased, but he still wore the cloak of grief that sometimes threatened to choke him.

Now was one of those times. He'd waited until the gorgeous man left his office before he fell apart and tried his best not to hyperventilate.

Use the skull-and-crossbones collar with the broken latch.

The boy who'd just left his office would have no way of knowing that—wouldn't have known that Damon kept that collar in his loft, had fixed the latch right after Jesse died because it was one of the only things he could do.

Damon wouldn't be able to use the damned collar on this boy—Jesse knew that collaring meant something—that it didn't happen on a first night together.

You don't even know the boy's name.

He shuddered involuntarily that he'd thought of him as *the boy.* Because that's what he'd called Jesse—and only Jesse.

Jesse had been the first to ever thaw what Damon had considered a heart of ice. First, and the *only.*

But something tugged at his gut.

He could've been lying. This could be part of an elaborate scam.

The only thing was, the man had definitely been military. A Ranger, like Jesse, or so he said. Damon didn't doubt it, had a nose for those things, having been in special forces himself what seemed like a lifetime ago. And the timing was exactly right. Jesse had died a year ago, nearly to the hour, although he'd lied to the boy about not having that information.

Fuck.

He called through the open office door, "LC, grab that guy who just left."

"I'm not your bitch," LC drawled, and no, LC was no one's bitch...not since Styx left. "And he's already in the lot."

"Dammit."

LC held his gaze for a second and then called to one of the bodyguards. "Renn—grab the guy in the brown leather jacket who just left. And bring a few guys—he won't come willingly."

LC didn't say anything more, didn't have to, and just headed to the front of the club to supervise. And Damon waited in his office, trying not to pace. Trying not to picture what the boy would look like, bound and spread for him.

Trying to pretend he wasn't hard at the thought of it.

He shifted but could do nothing to hide the erection in the pants he wore, and when LC barged back into the office, it was the first thing he noticed.

Thankfully, he didn't comment on it, just said, "They've got him and he's not happy."

"Makes two of us."

"Did he really know Jesse?"

Damon nodded. "He says that Jesse sent him here—wanted him to have a session with me."

LC's eyes widened, but wisely his mouth remained closed.

He was part owner of Crave, working mainly behind the scenes. He was also Damon's best friend—the only person Damon confided everything in. The only one he trusted enough to let him run the business in those months after Jesse died, when Damon couldn't get out of bed most days. LC had finally gotten him up and functioning.

Just then, the boy was dragged back in by three men—he was pissed for sure, but not fighting as hard as he could. Damon knew that, and whether it was grief or curiosity or both, he couldn't tell yet.

"Let him go," Damon commanded, and the men dropped him and left the room with LC, the office door shutting behind them as the boy stumbled forward until Damon caught him, held him hard by the biceps and stared at him again.

He was handsome as hell—all-American-looking, a blond haired, blue-eyed devil, even with his lips twisted into an angry grimace.

"What the fuck do you think you're doing?" The boy jerked out of his grasp and yes, he was strong. Damon had suspected as much. Earlier, when Damon had him by the shirt, backed against the wall, he hadn't flinched. It was the calm of a man who knew how to fight—who knew how to kill.

"What's your name?"

A jut of a chin, a glint of wild eyes and he ground out, "Tanner."

"Why did you come here?"

"Because I made a promise to Jesse when he was dying. I don't break promises like that."

"And you're willing to follow through on what he wanted."

Tanner pressed his lips together—he wanted to say no, that much Damon knew. For some reason, this handsome, strong, brave man wanted nothing to do with being Dommed, and it didn't appear to be for the usual reasons.

No, he wasn't uncomfortable, either in this club or with Damon and his leathers. But something was most definitely wrong with him.

"I'll do what Jesse wanted, yes."

"But you don't think you're man enough."

He waited for Tanner to snap an answer back, but none came. Instead, he shrugged.

"Well then, there's no time like the present. But no collar." He motioned for Tanner to follow him, out the door of the office, down a small hallway and into a room marked Room Four.

Once inside, Damon pressed a few buttons to bring the lights up and to remove the shading from the plate-glass divider that separated the room from the rest of the club.

As soon as he did so, the bar began to cheer. Damon activated the two-way speakers as well, so the sounds went from muffled to completely clear.

Tanner's eyes widened. "We're doing this here—where everyone can see?"

"Yes. That's what Jesse would've wanted."

Tanner couldn't have known that was the furthest thing from the truth—that Jesse understood the value of privacy at the start of a D/s relationship.

That Jesse would hate him for this.

Well, Damon hated Jesse for dying and leaving him. For refusing to quit the military and let Damon take care of him for the rest of his life.

For recognizing that Damon had been slowly dying inside during the last year of their relationship and continuing to satisfy his own needs instead.

18

Tanner swallowed hard and then he nodded.

Yes, let's see if this man is for real.

Chapter Two

Tanner pulled his focus off the crowd and back to what was about to happen in this room—and why. Focus had gotten him through a lot during his missions—it would have to do so again now.

Damon came up behind him, pulled Tanner's back to his chest in a quick move he hadn't expected. He started, readied for a fight but realized there was no need for one, not when Damon whispered in his ear, "I hope your ass is ready for this."

And even though his cock got harder thanks to Damon's touch on his chest, Tanner was pretty sure he'd never be ready for any of this—not the bindings or the crowds in this context. Not for that spanking bench with the restraints in the middle of the floor.

He'd been trying to push the panic from his mind from before he walked into Crave earlier—told himself to focus on the mission and forget the fear.

It had worked well, until now.

He knew the D/s relationship wasn't all about fucking, but in this case, it looked like that was exactly what would happen. He'd pushed that possibility from his mind, hoped for whips-and-chains shit—pain and control—but he'd never bottomed. The fact that he'd made a promise to start here, like this...

Damon might not fuck you.

He held on to that thought like a lifeline.

He'd been through far worse than what was to come tonight, hated that it could possibly break him.

He never should've come here.

Damon's hand was moving along his chest, pinching his nipples through his T-shirt and Tanner drew in a sharp breath. Took comfort in the fact that Damon was definitely hard too.

He heard "strip him" and "take him" and "fuck him" called out from the crowd, and his face flushed at the thought even as his body ached for it.

He didn't understand where the strange need was coming from, pushing up past the fear, but for the moment, he was grateful.

"Is that what you want?" Damon asked, and Tanner's throat was so dry he could barely swallow, let alone speak.

He had no idea what he wanted anyway.

"I asked a question," Damon said patiently, but Tanner knew that patience would be short-lived.

The thought of Damon's body covering his, holding him down, riding him, was too much to bear. This contact, even, was too much, considering he'd been home from his last tour for less than two days.

He was nowhere close to being ready.

But he'd waited too long to say no and Damon was done asking questions. He pushed Tanner off and commanded, "Strip, boy."

The words were harsh and somehow seductive at the same time. Tanner had no problem being naked in front of anyone...but doing this in front of a bar...Jesus fucking Christ.

He unbuttoned his shirt and yanked his jeans down. He rarely wore underwear when he wasn't working, and tonight had been no exception.

He heard the yells of approval, because yeah, he was hung like a motherfucker. He even saw the appreciation in Damon's eyes before they hardened again.

"Eyes down. Don't you dare look at me, boy."

Tanner did as he asked, cast his eyes down to Damon's black-leather-booted feet and felt his body flush.

"Walk to me. Eyes down."

Tanner followed the sound of his voice, let Damon's hands guide him farther and then down on his knees near the spanking bench. Damon knelt behind him, straddled Tanner's calves so that they were ass to cock again. For a few moments, Damon's breath lingered on his cheek as the man's hand roamed his chest. Pinched a nipple. Moved down to hold his cock, a thumb swirling the precome over the broad hood, and Tanner hissed and nearly shot his load right then and there.

Involuntarily, he pressed his ass back into Damon—the man was rock hard and Tanner heard a soft groan escape Damon when he ground his ass harder. He liked that he had some effect on the man who was threatening to undo him and so he did it again, until Damon rocked against him, the leather of his pants strangely erotic against Tanner's bare ass. The slow grind built faster, Damon tugged his cock harder and the crowd seemed to love every minute of the show.

It was all a show and still a moan drummed up in the back of his throat and escaped before he could stop it.

From Damon, there was only a soft chuckle that wasn't as friendly as it should've been. A strong hand on his back pushed him forward, breaking their contact and guiding Tanner into place before four locks bore down—one on each wrist and ankle, holding him effectively in place.

"It doesn't matter if you struggle, boy," Damon told him.

"This is bolted into the floor."

Tanner heard his own breathing harshen.

His legs were spread, and the apparatus he was chained to rotated in order to give his audience an angle of every single part of him. His ass was in the air, his dick jutting upward as his chest rested on the bench, and he began to sweat, a thin sheen that covered his body.

He pressed his forehead to the leather and tried to breathe. Felt Damon finger the cold lube against his asshole and he drew in a sharp breath, because there had been no warning. He willed himself to relax, waited for a finger to slide in, to open him.

But that didn't happen. No, Damon used a dildo—it wasn't large but it was knobbed—and worked it inside of him slowly as Tanner tried not to cry out. It hurt the way he'd known it would—he'd heard it was part of the draw for the bottom—the pinch of pain before the pleasure hit. But Tanner didn't like being this out of control, this vulnerable, and he wouldn't handle it well.

"You're tight, baby. You don't bottom much, do you?" Damon asked, but the question was rhetorical and Tanner noted that he went a little more slowly, used more lube. Tanner forced himself not to struggle against it—the sensation of being filled strangely erotic, but it fucking hurt.

Damon hadn't given him any kind of way to stop him, and although Tanner supposed he could make Damon cease all this somehow, he'd come this far. He would just fucking breathe and try to forget what was happening.

The hoots and hollers of the crowd made him keep his eyes closed.

For Jesse—that's why you're doing this.

But Jesse had been a good friend—a good teammate. Why

23

he'd want to put Tanner through this was beyond him at the moment.

"He's good at what he does, Tanner. So damned good. It hurts—and it's comforting at the same time. I can't explain it," Jesse told him.

So far, Tanner only got the *hurt* part. His ass burned, stretched uncomfortably, because he'd never had anything bigger than a finger in his ass...never thought he'd be bottoming to anyone, especially not like this.

And then the vibrations began, deep inside his ass, and he did groan, unable to help it. His hips moved and he rutted like an animal as the crowd cheered.

He opened his eyes, saw Damon's booted feet in front of his face. The man was sitting, holding the remote loosely between his own legs. "It's set to go off like this every twenty minutes. Let's see how much of a man you really are."

Fuck.

Tanner did not want to like this—didn't want to feel the sensations building inside, tightening his balls, making him groan, but a part of him was losing control and fast.

It wasn't supposed to go like this. Tanner figured they would talk—he would tell Damon about Jesse's last night. Jesse's last words. And then maybe, if they could get past that, Damon would do what Jesse had wanted.

He struggled to hold on, to not come, but it was impossible. The angle of the vibrating dildo was too perfect, slammed his prostate over and over with no relief. His cock was rock fucking hard and if he closed his eyes, he might even be able to pretend he was alone with Damon, that the tall, handsome man was the one taking him for a ride.

But a combination of willfulness, pride and stubbornness refused to let him escape into his fantasy even as he shot a hot throb of liquid all over the floor as the dildo continued to milk him dry.

The boy was beautiful. Rugged. Sensual. He hadn't minded getting naked—for good reason, since his body and his cock were the most perfect Damon had seen in a long time. He almost switched off the transparency lighting so he could have this one all to himself, because it had been so long.

But he wouldn't do that, no matter how badly Jesse might've wanted it.

You're a bastard for doing this to me. Those had been Jesse's first words to him during their first session, back when Damon was still actively Domming and Jesse had been in desperate need to be taken in hand, no matter how hard he fought it.

He shook the mental picture of Jesse out of his head—Jesse, splayed out and ready for him, begging him to stop until it was *oh* and *yes* and *fuck me now*—and he forced himself to concentrate on the boy in front of him instead of the one in his memory.

Tanner. *Say his name, dammit. Remember, this is not about pleasure.*

He spoke those words harshly to himself even as he remembered how good it felt to have Tanner grinding back against him, willing to take a submissive position even as he was convinced it was against his nature. And it would be so easy for him to kneel behind this boy, replace the dildo with his own cock, bury himself to the hilt. Would hear Tanner's moans, egging him on...and it would all feel too good. And he didn't want to feel good anymore—wanted to sell this place and all its memories, take his money and travel. This way, he could fuck nameless, faceless people, drift until it felt right, the way it once had a long time ago.

But for right now, he would fulfill Jesse's request and none of them would be happy.

Except this was not what Jesse would've wanted—not by a damned long shot. This wasn't what any sub should expect from his first time with a Dom, especially not a man fresh from some hellhole of a jungle with battle still fresh in his eyes.

Close the shades. Let him loose.

But he didn't, simply sat on a chair, the remote just out of Tanner's reach.

Tanner's back was broad, muscled... Damon should've been running his hands over the sweat-soaked skin, coaxing the orgasms out of him. Instead, he clasped his hands together and watched the boy struggle against his own will.

At first, Tanner kept his head down, but after he'd had his first orgasm—and what a sight that was to watch him writhe, helpless to stop his own primal urges from taking over—Damon ordered, "Head up, boy. Let everyone see that beautiful face of yours."

Tanner met Damon's eyes defiantly and then looked out into the crowd, knowing he was not supposed to look his Master in the eye without permission.

You are not his Master.

The boy—Tanner—was going to come again, whether he wanted to or not and Damon sat there and watched him struggle against the bonds. The transparency of the room and the harsh intimacy imposed on him had finally dawned as he looked out on the crowd, and his cheeks flushed as the howls directed at him grew louder.

"Damon's finally got a new boy."

"Damon's fucking him without fucking him."

"Look how much he loves it."

Tanner didn't love it—not completely. There was too much humiliation in this situation—too much confusion. And even so, the boy would not go down easily. He came three times. The fourth was a dry shudder of an orgasm, since he'd been milked beyond his capacity, and looked to be almost painful.

"Again," Damon said, prayed that Tanner would finally resist with words, would tell him no, to stop...to end this.

"I can't." Tanner ground out the words. Over an hour had passed, and although Damon had insisted the boy drink water, had held the bottle to Tanner's lips as he drank greedily, the climaxes were taking their toll.

And although *I can't* wasn't a safe word, it was enough. Because he hadn't given Tanner a chance to pick one. That was against everything he'd ever learned, everything he'd ever practiced, and it was the only way to ensure this man never came back to him.

He attempted not to hyperventilate, pushed the button for the privacy curtains and switched off the vibrator. Then he let Tanner out of the bonds. The man pushed off his knees then nearly dropped but grabbed himself quickly. When Damon attempted to help him, Tanner threw his hand off and picked up his clothes.

With the posture of a king, he opened the door and walked through the club bare-assed naked as Damon watched from the room's glass windows. And he did not look back.

Tanner had gotten to his car when a touch to his shoulder made him whirl around, arm up, ready for a fight. Didn't matter that he was buck fucking naked, his adrenaline and anger pumped to an almost unreasonable level, and any excuse to punch someone—or something—would've sufficed.

It was the man from the door—LC—and he was still not smiling. "You dropped this."

LC held out Tanner's wallet, which must've fallen out of his jeans when he was walking, wanting to get the hell out of the club but refusing to run. Tanner took it and nodded as he started dressing, shoved it into his back pocket and then zipped his jeans up. He didn't bother with the shirt, threw it into the car and prepared to follow it, to get the hell out of this parking lot and never come back.

"Damon's a prick," LC told him, his voice a drawl deep with anger. "That's not how it's done."

Tanner didn't answer him. Couldn't. Just nodded and got into the car and drove away from the club because he didn't know how it was done—but he was pretty sure that wasn't it.

You kept your promise. And fuck you, Jesse.

He pounded the steering wheel, not wanting to speak ill of the dead, and still the bile rose up inside of him at what had happened tonight.

You liked it. Most of it.

Jesus, he didn't know what end was up anymore. Just knew that his ass was sore, and he was half flying and half ready to cry like a fucking baby. And he wanted to be in the privacy of his own home.

It took him twenty minutes at top speed. He pulled into the garage, dropping his jeans as he walked toward the bathroom. He stopped only to grab the half-empty bottle of Jack Daniels, not bothering with a glass. Once in the bathroom, he started the shower, let the water steam the enclosed space before climbing in and shutting the glass door behind him. And that's when he let it go, the sobs ripping from deep in his throat.

At one point, he sank to the tile floor, kept the bottle out of the steady stream of water and took several deep gulps.

As the liquid burned his gut and soothed his soul, he wondered if it was ever going to stop hurting—if the nightmares would lessen. If maybe he wasn't cut out for this job the way he thought he was.

But he loved being a Ranger, had even been told he would be eligible for Delta Force training very soon.

But watching Jesse die...being unable to do more for his teammate than listen—and promise—well, that knowledge was slowly killing him. And even though he knew there was nothing he could've done differently, it still didn't bring the guy back.

You ruined Damon's life by letting Jesse die. And that was the painful reality. How could that guy have reacted any differently than the way he had?

Damon left the room as if it were a crime scene—in truth, it was—and went to his office, trying to shake the look on Tanner's face when he'd left from his brain.

Who was he kidding? It was burned on there—and he was practically shaking. A side trip to the bathroom and he lunged into a stall and threw up.

After a few minutes, he lowered his forehead to the cool tile, remembered doing this on the night he'd found out Jesse had been killed as well, not caring where the hell he was. None of these memories were good, and his stomach roiled again at the thought of what he'd just done.

Finally, he dragged himself up and out. He needed to shut down the computer in the office and head the hell upstairs to his loft and lock himself in and sleep all of this off.

But LC was waiting for him, arms crossed, looking more pissed than Damon had ever seen him.

"You're a bastard," LC told him without preamble.

"Fuck you," Damon shot back as he rooted around in the closet for mouthwash. He drank straight from the bottle and spit into the wastebasket to get the initial taste out—and then he grabbed his toothbrush and toothpaste and began to brush since it was apparent getting up to his loft would take longer than he thought. "Get the hell out of my office," he mumbled around the brush.

"It's my office too, asshole," LC said. "If Jesse sent that boy to you—that's how Jesse came to you, dammit. Or don't you remember the broken, lonely boy you tried to humiliate and push away? Just because Jesse refused to go doesn't mean you'll get lucky with this one."

He wanted to grab LC by the throat, shake him, but he refrained because LC was a hell of a fighter. "There is no one like Jesse—there never will be."

"So you're going to be a monk forever? Wear a hair shirt and do everything Jesse made you promise you wouldn't do, right? Because that's truly honoring his memory."

He hated when LC was right. Right now, he hated everyone and everything, including Jesse. He spit into the garbage can again and rinsed his mouth out with bottled water. Then he sank into his chair and ran his hands through his hair as LC watched him in sympathy.

He hated that too. "LC," he began tiredly.

"He's connected to the man you loved. How the hell could you have treated him like that? How the hell can you treat anyone who comes to you to learn about being a sub like that?"

He shook his head wearily, mainly because he didn't know himself. His nerves were taut, emotions frayed, and he would go over the edge and do something—or say something stupid to LC if the man didn't go away now.

LC knew too—Damon had known him for a long time. Long enough that subtlety wasn't something either man bothered with, and so LC slammed a piece of paper on the desk in front of him with the slap of a palm. Damon didn't look at it until the LC left his office

He remained brooding there at his desk for the next hour. Pulled out and stared at the picture of Jesse he kept in his desk drawer. Tried to figure out what the hell Jesse had been thinking.

And while he couldn't ever really know that, thanks to LC, he had the most important thing—Tanner's address.

He headed to his truck and drove around aimlessly for a while, radio blasting, wondering why the hell he would do this when he'd successfully gotten the boy out of his life.

Because you owe Jesse. Or Jesse owed you. Whichever way it was, Damon knew he'd get no rest until he made Tanner an offer...and an apology. And so he pulled in front of the address he'd programmed into the GPS, the soothing female voice telling him he'd arrived at his destination.

It was the right place—a townhouse near the base, nicely groomed. No car in the driveway but Damon hoped it was in the garage, wanted the boy—Tanner—to be home.

He stared at the house, his nerves still jangled. They'd been that way after his first meeting with Jesse as well.

Jesse. It had been so complicated. And at first that had Damon jumping right in and helping. Fixing.

Losing himself in the process until he didn't know who he was or what he wanted anymore.

Had he ever?

Jesse. Big brown eyes. Biting wit. And a need for submission as big as the state of Texas, where he'd been born.

Jesse had come to the club to survey the scene, check things out and, most of all, to find Damon, who, at his peak, was one of the best and most coveted Doms around.

He'd initially refused to play with the beautiful boy with the aching need in his eyes, knew how much work it could be to train a new sub.

"I'll do whatever you say," Jesse had told him earnestly, but the boy had the devil in his eyes.

Damon remembered frowning, saying, "They all tell me that."

But he hadn't refused.

It was supposed to be one night. One time with Jesse strapped to the spanking bench, writhing under the weight of Damon's hand, the steady slaps bringing him into subspace far more quickly than Damon could ever have anticipated.

Under the weight of the memories, Damon felt sluggish, like he could easily drown. The man in the house could be his lifeline...or could sink him even further.

Without knowing which, Damon got out of the truck and headed up the walk, rang the bell and waited. A long four minutes later, just when he was about to walk away, Tanner answered the door, dressed only in a pair of low-slung sweatpants. His eyes were red-rimmed and that tore at Damon's gut.

Tanner's chin jutted stubbornly when he saw Damon, his eyes blazed and yeah, Damon deserved it and the anger of Tanner's first words.

"How the fuck do you know where I live?" Tanner demanded.

"Your wallet."

Tanner went to close the door but Damon's hand shot out, stopping it. "That wasn't a proper scene," he started.

"Felt pretty real to me." Tanner's voice was hoarse, and he still held the door half closed.

"If it had been proper, you wouldn't have been alone. I would've been there to help you through it. I would've been there afterward, when you fell apart."

"Yeah, one night and you would've been able to put me back together, right?" Tanner's voice held the bitterness Damon had expected, but the boy didn't deny that he'd fallen apart. Instead, he let the door go and Damon pushed it open fully and took a step closer.

"I can do better. Give you what Jesse wanted you to have," Damon offered, his voice quiet.

Tanner flicked a surprise gaze at him. "You want another chance?"

"Not at the club. At my place. Just the two of us."

"I don't think...I don't think I'm cut out for this," Tanner admitted.

"There's more I want to know...about Jesse."

Tanner was still guarded, but he was a man of his word— Damon was counting on that...needed to make all of this right somehow.

"I can do that. The rest...I don't know," Tanner said.

"Why?"

"Look, it's not my scene, all right? I'm not a sub. I'm not a bottom."

Damon stared at the boy as the picture of him bound and spread and coming flashed before his eyes. He'd been out of the game for longer than he'd realized. That—and the fact that

Jesse had clouded his judgment—because he should've realized from the second he'd met the boy that Tanner thought he was a top. Damon knew, from the second he met the unarguably alpha male, that he wasn't. How to convince him was another issue in itself. "You sure about that?"

Tanner shrugged like it was no big deal, but the casualness of the gesture didn't match the confusion in his eyes. "Yeah, I am. Nothing wrong with it, though. I just prefer being in control."

Damon leaned in and put a hand around the back of Tanner's neck, waiting for the man to resist.

He didn't, and Damon rubbed the heated skin, still damp from a recent shower. He pulled Tanner a little closer although the boy tugged back a little.

Damon tugged harder, told him, "No, baby—you'd prefer someone to take all that control from you until you're moaning like a sweet little bitch."

Tanner's jaw dropped and his eyes glazed slightly, like Damon had just revealed his deepest, darkest fantasy. All Damon needed to do was to step back a little and glance downward to see that Tanner's cock had turned traitor. When Damon dragged his eyes back to Tanner's face, Tanner's cheeks had flushed in tandem.

It was all he could do not to take the boy inside and fuck him on the floor, but he let his hand slip away from the boy's neck reluctantly. "It's nothing to be ashamed of."

"No," Tanner agreed, not believing it, rubbing a hand along the back of his neck where Damon's hand had been. And he was still hard. "It's just something I'm not."

Tanner would insist that until Damon proved it otherwise, so for now, he didn't press it. "That's why it was hard for you to walk into the club and submit."

"Well, that and bringing up Jesse." Tanner shook his head as though saying the name was as hard for him as it was for Damon.

"You were close."

"We were on the same team. Leave no man behind."

"You didn't leave him behind, Tanner."

Tanner didn't answer and Damon knew that, no matter what he told the boy, he'd believe he somehow let Jesse down.

Damon knew that better than anyone. "Tomorrow night—after midnight. My loft's above the club—you can use the private entrance in the back. Be prepared to stay the weekend."

He turned and headed back to his truck before Tanner could say anything, before he could turn Damon down, because suddenly Damon wanted nothing more than Tanner.

Chapter Three

The music was loud, the rooms dark, and the Underground was just what Tanner needed tonight, his cock half-hard from the second he walked into this club that was nothing like Crave. The crowd was typically out of control and bad shit could happen to men who weren't careful here.

Tonight, he didn't feel like being careful. That in itself was dangerous but his adrenaline—his need to erase last night and Damon from his mind—made him race to the point of not caring.

He needed pleasure and if that had to mix with pain to satisfy him, so be it.

Pain brought him back to Damon—the spanking bench and how hard he'd come and how much he hated both himself and Damon for it. How his sleep was broken with dreams filled with Damon instead of his usual nightmares about Jesse's final hours. It had been something of a relief to wake up sweating and tangled in the sheets and coming...although having Damon's name on his lips made him angry all over again.

Damn, he needed a drink and another orgasm—not necessarily in that order. But the drink came at the same time the men started to circle and Tanner downed some beers and more than his share of shots so he could try to stop thinking.

Sometime between this morning's dream and the

afternoon's grueling PT session, he'd decided that he'd done what he could for Jesse, that it wasn't his fault Damon screwed up last night and now wanted another chance to help him fulfill the promise.

He was through with second chances and he'd been here more times than he cared to count. This was a, *don't ask, don't tell,* literally underground club—dark, anonymous, and it used to be the best place for Tanner to wash away his troubles.

He came here tonight to lose himself. If he could do that, he could prove to himself that he didn't need Damon and his bullshit pity offer.

The strobe lights and dance music had no place here—no, this place was strictly down and dirty. Some local town kids came here too, hyperaware of their sexuality and sometimes too impressed by the military men, although they'd be too gentle for what Tanner needed and so he ignored them.

He was cruised hard by several men—although some might recognize him as a top, many of them claimed to want to be his daddy.

It made him think of Damon's words and Tanner was glad no one could see his face burning in the dark.

"No, baby—you'd prefer someone to take it all from you until you're moaning like a sweet little bitch."

His cheeks heated as he thought of how he'd jerked off after Damon left, hearing Damon repeating those words to him, feeling the man's hand on the back of his neck.

Damon repeated the words to him in Tanner's dream too, and in that dream, he'd let Damon take everything.

"Fuck," he muttered, and one of the men standing close laughed and told him, "That wouldn't be a problem for me."

Tanner felt the man's hand run along his denim-clad hip

and he didn't pull away, let the man caress him as he drank another whiskey and scanned the club for familiar faces.

Joe and Hunt were here—his stomach tightened when he saw them both at the other end of the bar, circling a younger, no-doubt unsuspecting guy. They'd been together for a long time, although the only ones who'd know that were the ones who visited here. They hid their relationship well, as a necessity, since both were in the Army as well.

Jesse had done the same. Tanner knew Jesse was gay because, well, he *knew*. Being bi gave him the same gaydar, although Jesse appeared as butch as the next guy. He'd just looked young, even though he'd been a few years older than Tanner.

Jesse had been comfortable enough to confide in Tanner as well.

"I don't...I'm not enough for him," Jesse had said about Damon that night he lay dying in the jungle. "He needs more."

Tanner hadn't understood that at the time, just thought that Damon had sounded like an asshole. "Maybe you're just going through a bad time."

"Nah. He's just too good to me. I'm the selfish asshole who can't let him go." Jesse had closed his eyes. "I knew it would take this to do it."

"Dammit, Jesse, don't talk like that." Tanner had pushed him to open his eyes, to fight.

But Jesse had no more fight left in him.

Now, Tanner blinked, realized he'd gone back to the jungle in his mind far more easily than he'd wanted to.

He hadn't told Damon any of that, maybe he never would. Right now, he still agreed with his original assessment of Damon as an asshole. But he didn't know what went on behind closed doors. Two sides to every story...and Tanner didn't want to know either of them.

He had enough troubles of his own. His family wasn't happy with his lifestyle, and by lifestyle, they'd meant continuing to stay in the Army. The bisexual thing was something he'd no doubt take to his grave. He knew what his family's limits were, had learned long ago about keeping the truth from people for their own good.

According to Damon, Tanner was keeping the truth from himself as well. And while he didn't want to believe the truth in that at all, he did know that right now, he was in no shape for women. He would be too rough. But these men in the club, that would work for them.

After finishing his drink, he worked his way to the back room and found several willing men, one of whom got on his knees, unzipped Tanner's jeans and took his cock in his mouth without saying a word.

The man knew what he was doing, deep-throated him first, and Tanner rested his head against the wall and let the sensations of the man's sucking take over everything. Then he threaded his hand through the man's hair and forced him to work to his rhythm...hard and fast, because he didn't want to draw this out.

There were no connections to be made here. Tanner had always believed that's what he'd been meant for—a life of fucking and going home alone.

He'd been okay with that until last night—and now he couldn't get Damon out of his goddamned mind. Could feel Damon's hands on him still, flashed back to the scene at Damon's club and got harder, which seemed impossible.

"Fuck yeah," he murmured to himself as the talented mouth sucked him and a hand caressed his balls. He gripped the man's hair and his cock went down his throat again. He groaned, closed his eyes and imagined it was Damon.

Wouldn't that be something—Damon on his knees in front of him, taking his cock. Maybe even in front of everyone in the goddamned club, and the men would be cheering again as Damon held his hips tight and sucked and licked until he came down the man's throat.

That would never happen. And still, it was the dream he'd had last night, the one that made him wake up shooting and crying out Damon's name.

It confused the hell out of him. Damon had treated him like crap—and he'd allowed it—for Jesse.

But the man currently on his knees in front of him was treating him very well. His tongue caressed the bundle of nerves on the underside of his cock while he stroked, and then he sucked hard on the head and that was all Tanner needed. He shot down the man's throat, heard his own harsh breaths above the din.

When he pulled out of the man's mouth he was, as usual, still rock hard.

"Viagra?" the man on his knees asked as he stared between his cock and Tanner's face. "If not, that's just damned impressive."

Tanner didn't answer, just hauled him up and shoved him, chest against the wall.

The other man didn't protest, instead helped Tanner puddle his jeans around his calves. Tanner pushed his own jeans down low on his hips and rolled on the condom.

"I'm already lubed," the man said over his shoulder as he gripped the wall. "Go ahead."

Tanner drove into him, the man moaning about how good

he was, how big, and Tanner wanted to gag him because he didn't need the goddamned accolades. He just needed to come.

He closed his eyes and bit the man's shoulder through his shirt, wondering if Damon ever let himself be fucked...imagined no, and still pretended this man was Damon and that he was making the Dom crazy by fucking him at just the right angle. He would hit Damon's prostate over and over so he jumped and squirmed, but was unable to get away because he was impaled in that oh-so-fucking-good way.

Tanner had never let himself be fucked, but he'd been told by many that he was a hell of a fuck.

His balls tightened and he shot his load into the condom as the man's ass pulsed around him, and it wasn't enough.

It was never enough, and he pushed the sweaty hair out of his eyes and downed another beer and thought about going home.

Rethought going to Damon's and decided that could never happen.

But still, maybe Damon was right. Maybe Tanner did need to be fucked...but he'd be damned if he let Damon be the one to do it.

He swung around and saw Hunt and Joe watching him. Now that would be courting trouble. And trouble was what Tanner needed, with a capital T. Because if he wasn't making shit harder than it needed to be, then all wasn't right in his world.

He left the man, pulling up his pants, and went back to the bar.

"Hey." Hunt sidled up near him as if on cue, pushing a whiskey at him. "I saw you having fun in the back."

Is that what it was supposed to be? To Tanner, it was just

41

fucking and it hadn't helped relieve anything one damned bit. So he shrugged and gulped his drink.

"Joe and I can help," Hunt offered. "We know what it's like."

These men would be rough with him and he could be so back. Tanner wasn't a virgin in any sense of the word but that one. Bi and sexually curious from a young age, he learned to explore what he liked...knew that sometimes, pleasure mixed with pain could get him off nicely.

He also found that men got him off in a far different way than women—well beyond the obvious differences. Men were coarse and crude, and he could be far rougher with them—and they with him.

He found, after a time, especially after combat, he craved the rougher touches. Now, the only touch he craved was Damon's, and he didn't want that at all. "I don't want to be fucked," he blurted out, and Hunt laughed.

"Come on—we've got a room. It's about time you joined us."

Joe and Hunt had been together for a long time—Dom and sub, and they liked to play with others.

Tonight, he'd play.

Damon had slept through all of the next morning and afternoon and part of the evening, letting his stress and grief and guilt get the better of him. He finally got out of bed and showered around ten, was just making something to eat when LC knocked and then let himself inside, a handy trick he'd learned years before when living on the streets meant being able to pick locks to survive.

Now, LC had the loft on the other side of the club.

"LC, you've got to stop the breaking-and-entering shit,"

Damon told him.

"Fuck off." He was carrying bags of food and joined Damon in the kitchen, unpacking the containers from the restaurant around the corner and shoving Damon's sandwich aside.

Damon didn't argue. He took a few bites of the pasta meal and drank from the bottle of water LC put in front of him, all in relative silence. But those few minutes were all LC would give him.

"You're in a bad place."

"Yes," Damon agreed, then continued eating because it was easier than explaining. But then the meal was finished, as was the water and there was nothing left to do but talk it out. "This boy—Tanner—he's broken, like Jesse. I can't do this again. I can't fix another person, but I'll let him keep his promise to Jesse. I owe him that much after everything I did to him last night."

"Yes—I've had several people ask me if there's going to be a repeat, command performance," LC said wryly. "And Jesse might've been broken, but he was easy."

"Easy?" Damon snorted.

"Yes, because he knew what he wanted. This boy has no idea at all. No clue what he is or what he wants. This one...if you want him, you'll have to chase him."

He really hated when LC was right. Which was, unfortunately, too damned often. "I don't want him. I didn't want his goddamned address but I found him and invited him here for the weekend—told him to come tonight after midnight. I'll make it up to him but I don't want to talk about it." Damon slammed a hand on the table to end the discussion and LC remained unimpressed.

"He's going to get himself into trouble before then."

"What are you talking about? It's not even eleven."

"He's at the Underground. Fucking everything that moves...and he's going to get himself into trouble with the way he's feeling. Besides, Joe and Hunt are coming on to him pretty strongly...and you know how they like to drug the men who aren't exactly willing."

Damon's blood ran cold. He knew that LC had sources all over the club scene...he'd been as taken with Tanner as Damon had been, but for an entirely different reason. "You've been checking on him."

"He needs someone to. Apparently, Joe and Hunt have been after him for years. Tanner's always refused—would rather fuck everything and everyone in sight. But when the bartender at the Underground spoke with Joe earlier, he said he thought Tanner was warming up to the idea of being with the two of them."

"Tanner has no idea what that would entail."

"You're right," LC said as he stood to leave Damon's loft. "But it's not your problem, is it?"

Tanner and Hunt moved into the VIP area of the bar before going to the private back room. Joe was already there, holding court, but Hunt stuck close to Tanner. Bought him a couple of shots of Jägermeister, sucked on his neck as Tanner downed the shots and then Hunt ran his tongue to Tanner's lips.

"You and Jäger are a good mix," Hunt murmured, brought yet another shot up to Tanner's lips and man, he'd hate himself in the morning, for many different reasons.

None of that mattered. He was living for the moment, and Hunt's hand on his jean-clad cock was making that really easy.

"Glad you finally agreed to join us," Hunt told him, and

Tanner wondered where the sudden spike of his arousal came from...and the dizziness.

Jägermeister was some strong shit but he was no lightweight. He grabbed for the bar but Hunt was there, arms around his waist, steadying him. Kissing him until he was aware of the murmurs all around...knew they were being watched.

"What did you give me?" he muttered to Hunt when he came up for air, but Joe was there with them, suggesting to Hunt, "Why don't you take him back and let him get comfortable?"

Angry and horny all at once, Tanner let Hunt guide him through the small maze of hallways to the back room they'd rented. It was so hard to keep his thoughts straight, and they jumbled further every time Hunt tweaked one of his nipples or whispered that he couldn't wait to get Tanner's cock in his mouth.

Finally, they were in the private room.

"Ever been back here?"

Tanner shook his head, looked at the various implements lining the walls—dildos, floggers, masks—and it was all private and yet somehow way more intimidating than the room at Crave.

"I think I should go, Hunt," he whispered, his throat suddenly dry as hell.

Hunt handed him a bottle of water. "Don't worry so much— you're gonna love it. You know you need it. Come on."

Hunt urged him forward toward the bed, and Tanner let his knees buckle gratefully, sat on the edge and drank the water. Hunt stood in front of him, tugged off his own T-shirt, and then he moved to strip Tanner of his. Pushed him back and yanked off his boots and jeans as well.

The buzz of the drug though his veins was so...odd. He knew he shouldn't be here, but his arms were around Hunt then and they were rolling together on the big bed—nipping, sucking at one another. Tanner's cock leaked as Hunt stroked it slowly.

Too slowly. Impatiently, he pushed Hunt down and mounted him to fuck him.

But strong hands landed on his shoulders, massaging him with callused palms. "You're so ready, aren't you?"

It was Joe. He turned his head to agree and then Joe kissed him, hard and fast and before Tanner knew it, he was sandwiched between the two men on the bed.

His body was so fluid, and while Hunt sucked his cock, Tanner didn't much care what Joe was doing to his arms and his legs.

It was only when Joe turned him to his stomach and he realized he was bound and spread that he knew it was a bad idea.

He struggled, but that's what Joe and Hunt were after...that's what turned them on.

"He's ready," he heard Hunt murmur, and the room spun a little.

Tanner was hazy as to why he'd originally agreed to come back here...something about proving to Damon that he could do this whole D/s thing...that he was strong enough. But now, utter panic threatened to seep through the haze of drugs and hard-ons. Whatever they'd given him made him horny as hell—but he didn't want it from them.

Would've been helpful to come to that realization before he'd been cuffed, though.

Fuck.

He tried to act coherent and commanding, but all of that, just like all of this, was an act. "Joe, look—" he started now, but Joe didn't let him finish his thought.

"You're not owned, so for tonight I own you." Joe ran a rough palm across his ass, slapped it, then told Hunt what he wanted. "Give the baby boy some water to make him feel better."

Tanner refused to open his mouth, knew they were trying to drug him more and he'd had enough. He rubbed his lips against the sheets after Hunt pulled the bottle away. "What the hell are you talking about, being owned?"

"You don't have a daddy or a master, so you're a free agent. And you're a big-enough boy to know what you were signing up for."

Tanner's gut clenched. The terror was building fast now, and he staved off the panic attack, although just barely. Through gritted teeth, he asserted, "I told you, I didn't want to be fucked."

"And I never agreed to your terms." Joe ran another rough hand through Tanner's hair and let it trail down his back. Tanner's dick was responding, his body turning traitor and Joe knew it. "Don't worry—when Hunt and I get through fucking you, you'll be begging for more. They all do."

"Joe, let me the fuck up," he growled, and Hunt laughed softly.

"This is gonna be fun. I hope he screams," Hunt said and Tanner thrashed on the bed as Joe continued, his voice firm.

"I'm going to own you, Tanner. Hunt and I need a regular third and now, you're it. We're going to take you together...two cocks in your tight, hot hole. You're not going to know what to do with yourself once we're both inside of you."

Tanner fought a moan—less arousal and more fear because

47

that's what they wanted. His head swam, and he struggled harder, even as Joe ran his hand along the crack of Tanner's ass, fingering the sensitive flesh. "I can't wait to eat your ass...I'm going to take this patch of hair and suck on it until you scream. And then you'll bury your face in my ass and eat it until I tell you to stop. You're going to spend hours between my legs, boy."

"He's only doing that with me."

Tanner's heart leaped at the sound of the deep growl, and even though humiliation burned deep inside of him, he had no doubt that Damon was his savior.

"You can take a turn," Joe offered the Dom, and Tanner turned his head to watch the exchange, saw Damon dressed all in black and looking like a guardian angel sent from hell, a scowl on his face that Tanner was pretty sure was meant for him.

"He's mine," Damon repeated.

"He wasn't acting like yours—or anybody's—when he was fucking in the back room."

"He's allowed to do that," Damon said calmly. "Not this. "

"I guess he doesn't follow your orders well at all," Joe said and Tanner thought about how well he'd followed Damon's orders last night...how being tied down then was so different than this, even though he'd hated Damon for it.

Yeah, that's right—why was he looking to Damon to help him through anything?

Because you have no choice.

"Get your hands off him," Damon told Joe through clenched teeth. "I don't answer to you."

But Joe wasn't backing down. "Maybe the great Damon retired from Domming because he couldn't hang on to his boys.

But I can—and I will. Now get the hell out of my room." At Joe's unrelenting stance, Tanner's stomach lurched.

Damon had no real ties to him. There was no reason for him to start a fight when he could walk away. And if Damon couldn't get him out of this...

Tanner began to struggle against the bonds again, heard the bed creak and the binds bit his wrists. He didn't care—agitation made his throat tighten...until he felt a hand on the middle of his back.

"I've got you, sweet boy." Damon's voice was husky. Kinder than it had been moments earlier.

Save me, Damon.

He just didn't realize he'd said it out loud.

Chapter Four

When Damon had stormed his way into the Underground's private rooms and bribed his way into Joe and Hunt's room, he hadn't expected to discover Tanner tied up, spread-eagle on his stomach. The sight of the boy, bound with locked, heavy leather cuffs strung together with heavier chains, legs spread on the king-sized bed, so vulnerable and so fucking hot, took his breath away at first.

Tanner's skin was golden. Smooth, with hard muscles, his ass spread...although, at the moment, he was nowhere close to willing.

He could bury his face in that ass, eat it until the boy screamed with pleasure...but he'd already taken the boy publicly and that had gone poorly, and the sight of Tanner struggling against the bonds broke his heart. He rubbed Tanner's back to calm him and it worked momentarily, but he could understand the boy's panic.

This was a back room meant for play. Beyond the bed, there was the swing suspended from the ceiling, a wall lined with different floggers. Dildos and plugs, presumably from Joe's private collection, and no doubt Joe planned on using them inside Tanner tonight.

Damon knew that getting into a pissing match with Joe and Hunt was never a good idea. Joe had always been an asshole, wanting Damon's status but unwilling to extricate himself from the military in order to do so. He'd been with Hunt for years, the two men picking up boys and fucking them on a regular basis until they broke them.

Getting Tanner out of here in his condition, unscathed, could require a major ass-kicking. Damon was more than willing to do so, especially after he realized that Tanner had in fact been drugged as LC had suspected, judging by his sluggishness and the size of his pupils. And Joe eyed him as Damon continued to stroke Tanner's back. "Thought you were in mourning?"

"You shouldn't think. I wouldn't want you to get hurt."

Joe lunged and Damon stood to greet the gesture, taking his hand from Tanner's back momentarily.

"This is my room," Joe said with a snarl.

"With my boy. And you don't own the club."

Joe took a step back, crossed his arms, stood over Tanner proprietarily. "If he's yours, then prove it."

Damon bent to place a hand on Tanner's neck since the boy's breathing had become harsh again. "I don't take orders from you, Joe. You can see how he responds to me."

Tanner did respond as if he'd been Damon's forever—that was obvious to all of them. Damon watched Tanner's back rise and fall unevenly, smelled the fear and arousal mixing.

To Joe, that fear was intoxicating. "Maybe the four of us could work something out."

Damon would need to diffuse this situation quickly. "I need to speak to my boy alone for a moment—can you give us some privacy?"

Joe looked disgruntled, but he motioned for Hunt to follow him into the large bathroom. "You've got until Hunt makes me come."

When the bathroom door closed, leaving the two men alone, Damon knelt by the side of the bed and forced Tanner to look at him.

"You're here—drunk. Vulnerable. You let them drug you. You let your guard down, Tanner. Why is that?" Damon knew why—it was his fault. He'd stirred something inside Tanner that made all of this come up like a swirling sea of sand. "What are you doing here?"

"You're not my keeper," Tanner growled, his pupils larger than they should be and yes, that was true. He sounded very much with it and Damon just had to hope that Tanner's consent—when and if he gave it—wouldn't be the drugs talking.

Damon didn't think it would be. "I'm not your keeper, but you're damned happy to see me, aren't you, little boy?"

Tanner tugged at the bonds hard for a few seconds and then gave up, remaining still. Knowing Damon was his only way out and still being stubborn.

"You realize what they're going to do to you, right? And you being a top and all, getting fucked might not be what you'd planned. Or did you?"

"No. I've never been fu—" Tanner started and then stopped. Buried his cheek against the pillow and Damon's heart tugged.

How could the boy know if he was a bottom if he was still a virgin? No wonder Tanner was confused as hell. Damon had assumed he'd bottomed for men who didn't know what the hell they were doing, but this was an entirely different situation. "Last night...was that the first time someone put a dildo inside of you?"

Tanner nodded, his breath a hiccup.

"Okay, breathe, Tanner. Please breathe." Damon was telling

himself that too, because he was suddenly having trouble pulling air into his lungs. The boy was far too vulnerable here and Damon had been there himself and goddammit, he couldn't let Tanner's first time be here—not like this.

He'd tied men down for years—but there was nothing consenting about this situation. And still, there would have to be some sort of show to satisfy Joe. Tanner would have to consent to Damon. "I'm going to get you out...but I'll have to guide you through a scene."

Tanner protested by fighting the bonds so hard Damon was afraid he'd break his wrists. "Can't we just get the hell out of here?"

"There are rules. Protocol."

"Fuck your rules. You broke your own rules last night," Tanner spit out and yes, this was all about what happened last night. Tanner took what happened as the rejection it was. Damon hadn't realized how deeply it had affected him until this moment.

And still, he needed to talk some sense into him. "You're going to have to do what I say now."

"Forget it," Tanner said roughly.

"They're going to fuck you," Damon told him. "Do you want them instead of me?"

Tanner's breath hitched. "No. But I don't want to do this here with you...not like this."

"You have no choice."

"Please," Tanner whispered and his plea yanked at Damon harder than he thought possible.

There was a long moan from the bathroom and time was up. The bathroom door opened a few moments later, with Joe stumbling out on shaky legs and Hunt behind him with a self-satisfied look.

Joe leaned against the wall, said, "I'm waiting, Damon. Because if he's not yours—"

"I'm not yours either, Joe—so fucking untie me," Tanner demanded, and that's when Damon replaced his hand on the back of Tanner's neck.

"Stop, boy. Now. I know that I need to do this now. I have to show them that you're mine," Damon murmured. "Follow my lead."

"Fuck you," Tanner muttered, loud enough for Joe and Hunt to hear. Joe merely raised an eyebrow and then said, "I think someone needs a lesson."

For the first time that night, Damon actually agreed with him.

"Are you always this self-destructive when you come home from combat?" Damon growled in his ear, and Tanner realized he'd played with fire and would have to suffer the consequences—there would be no easy way out of this situation at all.

Lately, yes, he had been completely self-destructive. But he was humiliated and pissed and so fucking needy all at the same time, he didn't know what to say or do. Instead, he buried his face into the pillow again and hoped Damon understood, the way he always claimed to.

His arms were starting to go numb, as were his legs. The chains and cuffs were tight, and he was hot and cold at the same time.

"I'll undo the cuffs—but don't you move. Understood?"

The command in Damon's tone was something that couldn't be ignored. Tanner responded to it, wanted more of it, needed to obey and so he nodded, shivered as the cuffs came off. Damon rubbed the blood back into his arms and legs and Tanner allowed it, stayed calm and followed Damon's instructions.

"Better?" Damon asked and Tanner nodded mutely.

A smooth, cool palm rubbed the nape of his neck and Tanner breathed again.

"Touch is hard when you first come back," Damon murmured, so only the two of them could hear.

"It always was," Tanner whispered back. "Too much contact and I..."

"I know." Damon's hand rubbed, massaged, moved to Tanner's shoulders—that, he hadn't expected...he'd thought it would be all hard edges. No talking except for dirty words...no time for his likes and dislikes.

"Is it supposed to be like this?"

"It's not supposed to be like anything."

Tanner nodded. Swallowed hard. Then, "I like it rough."

"I know that too." But Damon didn't stop the gentle massage. His fingers trailed the dips of Tanner's muscles, even as Tanner's skin felt hot and tight.

He was achy and needy, ready to beg.

But he didn't. Wouldn't.

"You're a tough one, aren't you?" Damon mused. "All you have to do is ask."

"It's never that simple."

"This time, it is."

Could it be? He'd spent too much time believing otherwise.

"What do you want?" Damon's voice invaded his ears. "Do you want me to lay you out across my lap and spank you until your ass is red and you're coming on my thighs because you can't not come?"

Tanner opened his mouth to say no, but no didn't come out. His cock twitched though, his body betraying him every step of the way, and even though Damon couldn't see that, he knew. The man just knew.

"Spank you...and then fuck you into tomorrow," Damon continued and *God, yes.*

Tanner looked up when he realized he'd spoken those words out loud. Damon's eyes blazed, a small smile playing on his lips.

"Then it's going to happen. Now."

Within seconds, and with surprising ease, Damon pulled Tanner up off the bed and positioned him across his lap, bare ass in the air.

He cried out with a howl of surprise, struggled but a strong arm held him down, steadied him while the other came down, bare hand meeting bare skin. He swore he could smell the lust—his own, Damon's...Joe's and Hunt's, because even though he couldn't see them, they were watching this play out.

He heard his breath hitch and he felt like crying but he wanted more.

And then Damon's hand came down on his bare ass a second time and a third in quick succession. Tanner's face had already flamed, he lost his breath and began to moan incoherently. His body bucked, and he heard the sounds of approval around him as he lost himself in the rhythm...the pain...the loss of control.

He was going to come. His cock rubbed Damon's thigh and his balls tightened in anticipation, and he screwed his eyes tight and prepared to let his body take him where he needed to be. At least until Damon's voice broke in.

"You don't come without my permission—you know that," Damon told him firmly. "I think you just wanted to be punished."

"Please," he tried to say, but it came out a whimpered moan and that bought him three more heavy, fast slaps, and his cock throbbed against Damon's thigh. Then Damon grabbed his hair and lifted his head so Tanner could see Joe and Hunt watching, lust heavy in their eyes.

"Such a good boy...putting on a nice show for the men," Damon told him as he slapped his ass a few more times and Tanner struggled for balance. "Tell them you like it."

"I...like...it," he managed, and Damon put his head back down and continued without a break until Tanner lost track of everything but the all-consuming need to come.

"Now, Tanner. Come now or you're not allowed to come at all," Damon said suddenly and Tanner's dick listened, the orgasm spasming through him as though he hadn't come in months. The wet was on his belly and Damon's thighs, and he squirmed through the aftershocks as Damon stroked his ass, which burned like hell.

Slowly, he slipped down off Damon's lap. Again, he'd been put on display in front of people—and again, it was his own damned fault. And now he was on his knees with Damon embracing him...saw Hunt on his knees in front of Joe...and Joe's eyes on him.

The drug was wearing off now, thanks to the sweat...the activity...and even though his head wasn't completely clear of the drugs, he knew that his reaction to what Damon had done had nothing to do with drugs.

"I am going to fuck you, Tanner—make no mistake about that. But not here. I want you all to myself when my cock goes inside your virgin ass for the first time," Damon murmured so only Tanner could hear, and relief washed over him.

He buried his face against Damon's neck and he felt...stronger.

Damon murmured in his ear. "Why did you do this tonight, Tanner? Why not just come to me tonight—accept my invitation—"

The words he'd wanted to tell Damon earlier poured out easily now. "I don't want your house—I want the club. That's what Jesse wanted."

"Stubborn, stubborn boy," Damon muttered. "You're not ready for that. For this, even. Hell, I don't even think that you're ready for me in private—no, I know you're not."

To Joe and Hunt, their murmurs would seem nothing more than a Dom and his sub talking lovingly to one another. But Tanner's back was up again, all the familiar defenses rushing back. He pulled himself out of Damon's arms. "Don't tell me what I'm ready for."

Damon's face went stony and the gentle tone was gone when he commanded, "Then stay on your damned knees. We're not done yet."

Tanner hesitated only for a moment. Knew there was no way out now without ruining the entire act.

That's all it had been to Damon...an act.

He didn't want me...still doesn't. The whole "you're not ready for me" was no doubt Damon's way of cementing that.

Then I'll just make him want me.

Damon stood, moved Tanner so he was on his knees with Damon's leather-clad crotch in front of his face. And Tanner brought his mouth forward and kissed the soft leather and then licked, the taste mingling with fear and desire on his tongue as he looked up and saw the look on Damon's face...surprise and lust and oh yeah, he would make this man want him.

His undid the zipper slowly, pushed the leather down and away and gazed at Damon's cock. Ten inches, uncut.

"All for you, baby," Damon said, his voice husky.

He heard the appreciative murmurs of Joe and Hunt as Tanner slid his tongue over the broad head of Damon's cock, but he wasn't doing this for them. He wasn't even doing it all for Damon.

Damon, whose cock was hot, heavy…the skin like velvet against his lips. Tanner played with the bit of slick, tasting it, letting his tongue swirl it over the broad head as he stared up at Damon's face.

Goddamn, that did it. Damon was staring down at him, a look of utter pleasure on his face. Whether he wasn't able to hide it or he wasn't bothering to didn't matter.

Tanner wanted to be the one to put that look on his face again and again.

Damon leaned back against the wall, his cock twitching with an urgency he'd always prided himself on being able to control.

With Tanner, that didn't seem to matter. He rubbed the back of Tanner's head, his fingers tangling in the hair that would be too long for most military men but just right for a man doing covert ops.

A dangerous man. Right now, his mouth was equally as dangerous on Damon's cock. Because Tanner seemed to understand his pressure points, had learned quickly that Damon responded to a scrape of teeth across the fat mushroom head of his cock.

Damon jolted and he swore Tanner chuckled with his

mouth still full of cock, and so he tugged hard on Tanner's hair. Tanner simply did it again, then ran his tongue along the vein on the underside of his rock-hard cock.

Jesus—there was no way out of this one. Training Tanner to behave would be harder than he'd thought, and honestly, Damon had no desire at the moment to even try. Instead, he decided to let himself be thoroughly fucked by Tanner's mouth. If Joe and Hunt wanted a show, they'd get one.

Tanner was groaning around his cock now, and Damon fought the urge to fuck Tanner's throat, hard and fast...to get all of this over with and figure out how to stop Tanner from ever getting himself in this position again.

But the position Tanner was currently in was so damned good. Tanner was taking care of him, and that never happened. Being the one in control meant he would give all the care—and that usually got him off.

This was entirely different—this was Tanner kissing and sucking his way up the length of his shaft, burying his face in his balls as his cool palm wrapped and stroked Damon's length. He wished he could lie down and spread his legs and let Tanner go to town—could picture himself spread with Tanner's head bobbing between his legs.

God, he loved being sucked. Nothing better.

No one better than Tanner—he was sure of it.

He reached up and tugged at his own nipple under his shirt, pulling it to a taut peak as Tanner glanced up at him, swollen lips around Damon's cock, cheeks hollowed from sucking...a thumb giving just the right amount of pressure on his perineum to make Damon grip him more tightly by the hair.

That only made Tanner more ferocious on his assault.

Damon started as Tanner's tongue went in and out of his piss hole, fucking it with his tongue speared, making Damon nearly lose it. And with Joe and Hunt watching, the sweet boy turned into a man threatening to suck out all of Damon's control, and more easily than it should've been.

He heard moans and realized they were his, drumming up from the back of his throat and echoing loudly in the room as his hips rocked against Tanner's mouth. Tanner, who continued the sweet torture with his tongue and teeth.

And he was, for the first time in a long time, pretty damned helpless and hopefully doing a decent job of hiding it.

One glance over at Joe and Hunt told him it didn't matter—both men had glazed eyes and cocks out, stroking one another as they watched Tanner work. Any moment now, they would leave...or begin fucking in the doorway. It didn't matter. It would be his chance to get Tanner out of here.

But first, he would come. He glanced down at Tanner again, who'd closed his eyes as he sucked and tugged and teased, and yes, the boy was made for this. And then Tanner deep-throated him, as if he knew Damon would lose it soon. He closed his eyes and leaned his head against the wall as his orgasm shot from him, with Tanner taking every goddamned drop, his hands massaging Damon's balls as if milking it all from him, sucking him dry with great care. He shivered under the touch as he massaged Tanner's head, hands through his hair.

"Good...so good, sweet boy," he heard himself saying as Tanner's strong hands wrapped around his hips as he pulled himself up eye to eye with Damon. His face was flushed, his eyes glazed, and Damon knew that everything that had just happened between them—the unexpected intimacy—was way too much, too soon and they were both battling feelings they'd never expected.

Tanner leaned forward and kissed his neck as he carefully

tugged Damon's pants from where they'd fallen below his hips, zipped them and then remained with his forehead against Damon's shoulder.

They were both in so much damned trouble.

When the senior bouncer, Renn, came to get him from where he was holed up in Damon's office, LC knew immediately that there had been another attack. This would make the second in less than a week...and LC would have to tell Damon about it soon if they didn't stop.

Until then, he would handle them by himself. Had to.

He'd convinced himself that the first time was an unlucky fluke, a horrible incident that could've happened anywhere. That man, beaten, bruised, assaulted sexually, had refused to let LC call the police. His boyfriend had taken him home and LC and Renn and the others had looked around for hours, trying to find any traces of the assailant.

They'd come up empty. "Where did it happen?" he asked Renn.

"Alley. Same MO. Dammit, the new guy took a cigarette break and when he came back, he found the guy." Renn looked upset and rightly so. Whoever was doing the attacks was watching and waiting. A patient attacker. "He's outside with Jamie."

LC strode through the still-half-crowded club—it was last call and Renn hadn't wanted to rush everyone out and call attention to the assault.

When he got to the side door, he paused for just a second and then pushed outside, Renn on his heels.

The man sitting up against Jamie, another bouncer, had

been beaten—that much was obvious. His pants had been pulled up—Renn told him they'd been found down around his ankles and that he'd admitted to being forcibly sodomized.

"How're you doing?" LC asked.

"I'll be all right." But he wouldn't be. Not for a hell of a long time.

"Did you see who did this to you?"

The man shook his head. "It happened so fast. He found me out here and he dragged me to the corner. Put a rag in my mouth so I couldn't scream."

"I'm going to call the police."

"No." The man struggled to get up, despite the obvious pain. Jamie kept him in place to stop him from hurting himself.

"You need to go to the hospital to get checked out. And you need to make a statement."

"I need to forget the entire thing happened," the man said. "What are you worried about—I won't sue the club."

"I'm worried about you going home alone with a head injury," LC pointed out.

"My roommate will be there. You can call him." He rattled off the number and LC dialed and yes, the man on the other end of the line said he'd be right down to pick his hurt friend up.

In the meantime, Jamie helped the man inside to a more comfortable, private place and LC went into the office and paced until the club emptied completely and the man's roommate took him away out the back entrance.

The man never did give LC or any of the others his last name. Renn knew him as Daley, and whether or not that was a real first name or not was anyone's guess.

Damon must still be at the Underground with Tanner. LC

was happy for the small miracle, because he hadn't expected lightning to strike twice.

"You think we should call the police ourselves?" Renn asked him now, as they stood at the door of the office and LC stared out into the club, which only held bouncers and bartenders in the process of cleaning up. "We still have an obligation to the men who come to this club, even if that guy didn't want to do it."

They did. But LC couldn't bear involving the police in this. "Let's step up patrols along the alley, okay?"

Renn nodded, sensing the subject was closed.

None of the employees knew the extent of what this might entail—LC would keep it that way. "We don't tell Damon about this," he said forcefully, and Renn agreed and said he'd pass that along to the other men. They all knew Damon was just starting to make the climb out of the hole he'd dug himself when Jesse died. They didn't want to see anything push him back down.

No, LC could handle it, the way he'd handled it all those years ago. Why the nightmare was returning now, he had no idea. But it was, and LC would deal with it in the best way he knew how.

Tanner wasn't sure how long he remained pressed to Damon, but he became aware of Joe and Hunt fucking on the bed behind him, of Damon urging him to get dressed, and he peeled himself off of Damon.

He couldn't believe what he'd done. His mind swam, and he could barely get into his clothes. He tried batting away Damon's helping hand at first until Damon whispered for him to cut the shit because they needed to get the hell out of the damned club.

He relented. Thought about being tied down and scared before and that made compliance much easier.

"Back exit," Damon explained as he folded Tanner into his truck. "I'm assuming you took a cab."

"Yeah."

"Good. Then I'm taking you with me."

"Why?"

"Because Joe and Hunt know where you live. And where I live. And they'll be checking to see that I didn't lie to them." The truck pulled out of the lot in a fluid motion. Tanner wasn't even drunk anymore. The sex, the commands, were what had made him weak. And strangely sated.

"I'm too damned damaged for you. For anyone," he muttered. "You should be running."

"You really think I'll go that easily?"

"I don't know shit about you."

"But I know a lot about you. What your cock looks like...the way your face flushes when you come...the sounds you make..."

Tanner felt his cheeks flame. "I don't want to be anyone's challenge."

"You're more than that."

Tanner let those words sink in for a long moment as the truck flew along the near-empty highway.

"Why them? Why even give those men a chance of getting into your ass?" Damon asked finally, breaking the silence.

Because then it wouldn't have mattered. He could've proven to himself that Joe and Hunt weren't right for him, and that he was a top. "I'm not a submissive."

"You take command well," Damon said mildly.

"On the job, not with sex."

"Like when my cock was down your throat?"

"Damon, Christ."

"You give an amazing blowjob," Damon continued, unfazed. "I'd like to keep you between my legs all day. You can spend hours just sucking me."

"I wasn't exactly following your commands, was I? Because if I'm not mistaken, the great Dom Damon lost a bit of his control back there."

Damon simply smiled but Tanner took note of the way his hands clenched around the steering wheel. There was so much more to all of this than Tanner understood. And still, he didn't know if he would be able to stick around and see it all through.

Damon ushered him up the back stairs to the loft and didn't turn on any lights as he maneuvered Tanner to the bedroom. The streetlights left a soft glow through the sheer blinds on the windows. The music from the club had been thumping when they'd entered the building, but Damon's loft, his sanctuary, was soundproofed.

"I can go home," Tanner was protesting, but he was already stripping. Damon pulled the comforter down and practically shoved the boy into the bed, knowing he would be sleeping on the couch alone.

"Shut up and sleep. We'll talk when you wake up. You owe me that much," Damon said roughly, ignoring how badly his cock strained at the thought of getting into his bed with the boy and fucking him blind.

He could make Tanner want him right now—could easily make that happen, but it was too soon. The fact that Tanner wasn't arguing too fiercely about staying in Damon's bed after the spanking and the blowjob told Damon those boundaries were breaking down, but not quickly enough.

Tanner fell asleep within minutes and Damon watched him for a few moments, noting how young he looked...how there was still so much innocence in his face despite the hell he'd been through.

He looks damned good in your bed.

He was the first one who'd been there since Jesse.

Damon finally walked away, stretched out on the leather couch, which was at least comfortable, and caught some rack time. And when morning came a few short hours later, he got up to check on the boy and found Tanner gone. There was no note, no sign of him being here except the smell of him on Damon's pillows.

You're getting old if you couldn't hear him sneak out. In his heyday with Delta, the boy wouldn't have been able to get a pinky out of the bed without Damon knowing. And suddenly, he was tired of thinking, of old memories coming to haunt him, and so he slid into the sheets that were still warm and stayed in bed most of the day, getting caught in endless loops of dreams in which Tanner was splayed for his pleasure, with Damon's tongue up his...

"...going to get off your ass today?"

LC's voice carried over from the kitchen to the bedroom, and fuck it all, Damon needed to deadbolt the damned door to keep the man out. Damon shot him the finger but reluctantly rolled out of bed and into the bathroom.

"So, did you rescue him?" LC called, because he was like a dog with a bone, and he wouldn't be deterred until he had the entire story.

Damon grunted his reply as he took a piss. "I saved him. Brought him home to sleep it all off and now he's gone. End of story."

After he washed his hands and yanked on shorts, he came into the kitchen to find LC shaking his head, like Damon was hopeless. "You didn't try to stop him?"

"No. I didn't even hear him leave. Quiet little fucker." He heard the hoarseness in his own voice as he sat back on the couch and ran his hands through his hair, feeling beat up as hell. He hadn't been prepared for the swell of emotion that nearly toppled him.

"Shit, I'm sorry," LC told him. "I didn't want this to fuck you up more."

Damon snorted. "He would've been hurt if I hadn't gone. It was a stupid idea to think I could do this without messing it all up again, anyway."

"What happened between you two at the club?"

"He had to do something he wasn't ready for. Again, it's my fault. Damn you, Jesse." He buried his hands in his hair, felt LC sit next to him and sling an arm across his shoulder.

"Jesse knew you wanted to sell the club."

Of course. Jesse knew everything. The problem was, he never did anything about it. "I didn't want what Jesse did, LC. It was all too much."

It was the first time he was saying the words out loud—and he felt as if he were betraying Jesse, but he had to spill all of this out or it would break him.

He needed to move on.

LC waited a beat before he spoke and then, "I've known that for a long time too—probably before you did."

"Then why didn't Jesse do anything? How could he not have?"

"He didn't want to." LC's voice was hard now. "Look, I loved the guy too, but he was damned selfish when it came to his needs."

He had been. And Damon had felt there was no way to escape—partially because he'd still loved Jesse...and partly because he felt completely responsible for his charge.

"I thought maybe I could do it with the club, LC. But I'm done. Out," he whispered hoarsely. "Too many memories."

"I know. We'll sell, then figure out what to do next," LC said. "We always do."

Comforted, Damon let LC rub the knots out of his shoulders for a silent half an hour. LC, who'd been there for him for a hell of a long time.

The man understood what memories could do. When Damon felt better, he would take some time to remind his friend that he needed to crawl out of the weight of his own past as well.

When LC finished, he rubbed the back of Damon's neck. "Tonight's Dave's retirement party at Rex's. You're expected to go," LC reminded him.

He was—and he would go. "What about you?"

"Someone's got to stay and run the place," LC said. "I think you'd rather it be me tonight."

Chapter Five

After finally dragging himself up and out, Damon was having a better time than he'd expected at Rex's, mainly because he spent the first hour laughing at his Navy friend who was in love...and miserable as fuck.

"Tell him," Damon insisted as he lounged against the kitchen counter, staring out into the crowd of men out of uniform, a half-empty glass of whiskey in his hand.

"I can't. He's under me," Rex pointed out grimly.

"Yes, that's where you want him." Damon laughed at his own joke and ducked Rex's attempted slap to the head. The men had known each other since Damon was in Delta, and he and Rex had done some joint task force missions together.

"He's straight. And a total pain in the ass." Rex shook his head as he glanced at the man they were discussing, a Navy SEAL like Rex who defined tall, blond and handsome. "Sawyer goes out of his way to drive me crazy."

"Sounds like he's looking for your attention."

Rex took a sip of his beer and shrugged as if it didn't matter. "You think?"

"He's here, isn't he?"

"For Dave—it's his party."

"Keep telling yourself that, you dumbshit." But Damon

couldn't deny that he understood what Rex was going through. With some of these young guys, it was hard to tell if they were gay or not, and one wrong move could ruin a career. But judging by the way Sawyer kept glancing over at Rex, Damon was pretty certain he could see something there.

And then Tanner walked in and Damon finished his drink in one gulp, unable to deny the tug he felt on seeing the handsome boy. Rex, of course, noticed immediately.

"You know him?"

"He served with Jesse."

"Ah." Rex remained silent for a minute. "Something going on between you two?"

Damon was saved from having to answer that question by another.

"Need a refill?"

A young soldier, one who'd been scoping him out all evening, was by his side. Damon said no to the drink because he didn't need to hit the bottle tonight, but let the young man named Jordan flirt like hell with him.

Jordan was handsome. Receptive. Damon wondered if the young soldier would end up under him tonight. It wouldn't be hard to get Jordan to come home with him, to fuck him outside on the beach, even.

Jordan was not Tanner. And therefore, Damon couldn't mess up again, the way he seemed to every time he tried to make things right with the boy. Better to push Tanner away, once and for all, because he'd fucked up with Jesse and would no doubt continue to do so with Tanner. Making Tanner hate him would be better for both of them. He was sure of it.

This was the last place Tanner had expected to see Damon

mingling with the military men as if he belonged...and it was suddenly so obvious that he did.

Jesse had never mentioned that Damon served. And it wasn't like Tanner and Damon had spent a lot of time talking about anything but sex. And Jesse.

Damon was no doubt pissed at him for leaving so abruptly, but Tanner hadn't wanted to face the morning after. Could barely believe what he'd gotten himself into and hadn't wanted a lecture from the former Dom who'd literally saved him.

Still, he owed the man a thank you. But now, Damon was busy talking to a guy named Jordan, and smiling too damned much.

His friend Sawyer handed him a beer just then, told him, "Take a picture of that guy—it'll last longer."

"Shit." Tanner tore his gaze away and chugged half the bottle.

"I'm guessing you know him."

"Kind of."

Sawyer wisely didn't say anything more. Although notoriously straight, there was something that told Tanner there was a lot more under the man's surface.

The party was a mix of men—gay, straight, *don't ask don't tell* out in full force. Tanner figured he'd put in an appearance and take off and...

What? Go fucking?

But now that he saw the apparent interest in Damon's eyes as he spoke with Jordan, Tanner's stomach clenched. He didn't know Damon well enough to know if that interest was feigned or real.

Tanner wanted it to be faked so badly it hurt. He finished the beer and slammed it on the table next to him a little too hard.

"I've seen him look over at you a couple of times. Why don't you just go over there?" Sawyer asked.

"I can't." Tanner would have to harden his damned heart. He'd been doing what Jesse asked, not looking for the love of his life.

What did it mean that he'd even considered Damon having the potential to be a great love? In the space of a week—technically, only two nights—Damon had turned him inside out, had Tanner craving his touch.

Had him wondering how the hell Damon knew him so well.

You're not a goddamned bottom, he told himself fiercely, which didn't explain why he had dreams where Damon was buried to the hilt in his ass. In those dreams, Tanner loved every minute of it.

Dream Tanner was obviously an idiot. An extremely horny one that...

"You're not going to say hi?"

Damon's voice broke Tanner's reverie—he looked at the dark-haired man as Sawyer moved away and felt his cheeks heat. "I didn't know—"

"That I'd served?" Damon paused and handed Tanner one of the beers he'd been holding. "You did."

It was true...the commands inherent in Damon's tone had been what Tanner was used to. The way Damon held himself...yes, it was crystal clear now.

And it made Damon that much more attractive to him.

Tanner took a slug of the beer and then asked, "Are you taking that guy home with you?"

Damon raised a brow. "Why? Does that bother you?"

Tanner didn't answer. Couldn't. He just knew it did.

Tonight, he would dream of Damon and he'd wake up coming with Damon's name on his lips. And Damon was basically telling him that yes, the guy was going home with him, to his loft...the bed Tanner had slept in last night.

He'd wanted nothing more than to wake up next to Damon, had hoped the man would move into the bed with him. But when Tanner had opened his eyes and saw he was alone, that Damon had remained on the couch sleeping, he knew that all of this was simply a favor for Jesse.

And still, he heard himself asking Damon, "Take me home with you instead."

"If I do, you'll run again," Damon told him, pushed past him to walk away.

"You promised," he blurted out.

"I guess we've both broken a couple, so let's call it even," Damon said smoothly. Detached. Not the same man who'd had Tanner over his knee and then just held him.

Tanner hated feeling this lost. He resented the hell out of Jesse for making him make this promise, hated that he wanted Damon more than he'd wanted anyone in his life.

He moved closer to Damon, lowered his voice. "I'm having trouble, Damon. It's not my scene."

"Doesn't mean you can't enjoy a sample every now and again. Doesn't mean you can't learn something about yourself when you're tied down or spanked."

Tanner thought about the truth in that statement. He'd learned the fine line between pleasure and pain a long time ago.

"Submission is a gift," Damon continued. "I don't take that lightly."

"You did that first night."

"That night had nothing to do with submission. For either

of us." Damon paused. "Why do you fear the loss of control? Because you think it makes you helpless? Weak?"

"I was, with Hunt and Joe."

"That's because that wasn't submission. It's not about fear. It's about pleasure. Yours. You're the one who calls the shots. I can make you feel so good...can turn you inside out, upside down. I can have you begging me to fuck you, own you..."

Tanner didn't doubt it. The power of Damon's words alone were enough to make him practically come in his pants in the middle of a crowded party. "I don't want..."

"What?"

"All that whip-and-chain shit...I just want..." *Skin to skin with you. You holding me.*

When he couldn't finish, Damon did so for him. "If you can't say it, you don't get it."

"Jesus, Damon."

"What are you looking for from me?" Damon demanded, although his voice remained low and controlled. Two days ago, Tanner wouldn't have had an answer beyond fulfilling Jesse's wish. Now, the answer was more complicated, his body more than willing to do whatever this man wanted him to do.

He wanted so much...things he never thought he had wanted.

He wanted forgiveness. But how could he ever expect that from Damon when he couldn't even forgive himself?

Damon looked like he was about to reach out and touch him, but then he pulled back. Tanner realized that his skin prickled at even the thought of contact. "Are you this good? Do you make all the guys you're with want you the way I do?"

"Yes."

God, Tanner wanted him to be lying, wanted to be special

for Damon and hated himself for giving a fuck. His body was taut, aching to be pulled into Damon's... "Okay, then. I guess I'm going to get out of here."

"That would probably be best."

No, it wouldn't be, but Tanner didn't argue. Instead, he left without looking back, drove home and paced around the floor of his townhouse until he was sure he'd worn a groove in the floor.

If you go to him...

He shook off the thought, the fear that balled tightly in his belly, because that all fought with his arousal.

His cock won.

Damon could and would take him in any way he wanted. Tanner had known that from the second he'd met the Dom and still, he hadn't been able to stay away. He'd never thought himself capable of any kind of real feeling—not like this.

The fact that Damon dismissed him so easily and had left with someone else was too much for Tanner. Because as much as he wanted Damon to claim him, he knew he'd already laid claim to Damon and he wasn't giving him up without a fight.

Fighting was something he understood well, was as used to it as breathing. He'd been doing it his whole life.

Growing up with a silver spoon in his mouth never sat well with Tanner. He was always somewhere doing something he wasn't supposed to, whether it was fixing a car or hanging out with the staff...doing things that were beneath his station, as his mother would put it.

He'd refused boarding school even though he was the first in a long line to do so and went to public school instead. And the Army had been his escape, his salvation, a place where no one looked down on him for working with his hands or getting dirty.

He was made to be a warrior—he felt that deep down in his bones, never felt more comfortable or right than when he was in his cammies...at least he had, until Jesse's death had him reeling.

It shouldn't be surprising that it had taken a warrior like Damon to finally understand him. He didn't have Damon's file, but he could imagine that man on the missions that were so classified they never had a paper trail. He wondered if Damon was still plugged in enough to know that Tanner had been handpicked for Delta training, which didn't guarantee entrance to the elite ops team, but rather a chance to prove himself worthy.

He had a lot to look forward to, and if Damon could forgive him for Jesse's death...maybe then he could forgive himself.

A knock on the service door registered with Damon through his haze of sleep. As he dragged himself out of bed, muttering something about it being too late for someone to be visiting even though it was only midnight, he checked the camera and saw the cab leaving the parking lot and Tanner standing out in the hailstorm slamming his fist against the door.

The man had the nerve to be pounding angrily on his door? No, Damon was the angry one—had been enough that he'd left the damned party right after Tanner had...and had been alone when he'd done so. He'd bypassed the pounding music and the crowded club in favor of bed and had just fallen asleep when the knocking had awakened him.

He opened the loft door and went down the back stairs, the music from Crave a backbeat to his movements. When he shoved open the heavy back door, Tanner just pushed past him.

"What the hell are you doing?" Damon asked him as he shut the door against the freezing rain that was coming in sideways.

"What the hell are you doing?" Tanner challenged.

"Boy, you do not want to go there."

"Yeah, I do. I want to go there. Want to know why you acted like an asshole to me tonight."

"Wait—you're pissed at me?" Damon asked in a tone that would make lesser men stand down. But the man in front of him was not that way—never would be ordered around easily or well—and that boiled Damon's blood in a way that was both good and bad.

"What gave it away?" Tanner stood, unapologetic. Defiant. And then he advanced slowly. A predator, wet and hungry and unstoppable... Damon fought the ridiculous urge to back away, to head up to the loft and close the door and not let this boy—this man—in.

But Damon stood his ground as well, let Tanner come closer until there were mere inches separating them. And then, Tanner's hands went around him, yanked Damon against him and kissed him, pinning him against the wall like they were in the back room of a club. It was as if Tanner expected to turn and take him, to overpower him.

It wouldn't happen, of course. Damon would never let it.

But he could imagine it. Tanner could strip him, turn him, take him, right here against the wall. Damon could almost feel the heavy cock filling him until he cried out with pain and with pleasure—would let Tanner pound all the demons out of him. Fuck him blind.

God, he hadn't realized how badly he wanted that to happen until now and so, for the moment—for many long moments—he let Tanner kiss the shit out of him, grind their cocks together until he knew he could come in his pants and not care.

But he didn't. Instead, he turned the tables and pushed Tanner so the man stumbled back a bit. Breathing hard, mouth swollen and his clothing still soaked from his walk in the rain.

For the first time since Damon had let him in, Tanner looked unsure.

This time, it was Damon who advanced. "You demanded to come in. There are consequences to every action."

"So you're going to teach me a lesson?"

"One you should've learned a long time ago," Damon agreed. "I'm not a saint, Tanner. I rescued you from those men, but the sight of you like that..." Damon's voice was husky, rough with need and that hit Tanner's cock as surely as a hot mouth. "If you come upstairs, I will fuck you."

Damon's words were a promise, not a warning, and Tanner knew there was no turning back. His body trembled and that made Damon smile.

"You like my weakness," Tanner said, but Damon shook his head and murmured, "That's not weakness, baby. That's surrender—and they're not the same thing at all."

Tanner guessed he would soon find out if there was truth to those words. He'd come all this way, made this move, and now it was time to put up or shut up.

He began the long walk up the stairs toward the loft with Damon behind him, every step a surrender in itself. When he got to the top of the stairs and the open door to the loft, he paused at the threshold, but Damon didn't give him that luxury for long.

Instead, Damon pushed past him and then turned, pulled

Tanner in by fisting the front of his sweatshirt and yanking him inside. In a swift motion, the sweatshirt was off, hitting the ground with a heavy, wet thump that made Tanner jump.

"Easy," Damon murmured. "I've got you."

There would be nothing easy about this. "I thought you had company."

"I didn't bring him home with me."

"Why?"

Damon paused for a long moment and then said, "He wasn't you."

Tanner's throat tightened. And, as he stood there in just his wet jeans and boots, Damon tugged off his own black T-shirt and threw it to the ground. And then he unzipped the worn jeans—they hadn't been buttoned in the first place—and let them drop off.

He wore nothing underneath them and he was already more than half-hard.

If you come upstairs, I will fuck you.

"Do I need to undress you?" Damon asked.

Tanner was frozen, and it had nothing to do with the chill from the outside. Somehow, the intimacy of this setting versus coming in front of a club full of people was far more intimidating. Because he'd known that what happened between them previously was bullshit...but this—what was about to happen—was all too damned real.

And he was scared to goddamned death.

"We learned that fear is a good thing," Damon reminded him, as if reading Tanner's mind, and Tanner cursed his lack of a poker face with this man. Reached out and dragged Damon's naked body to his and kissed the shit out of him again, reveling in the fact that Damon responded. He wrapped his hand around the back of Damon's neck, pulled the man hard to him, and for a while they remained like that as Tanner ground against him, the sweet friction of his dick against the wet denim of his jeans nearly doing him in.

Damon pulled back and chuckled softly as Tanner kept his hand on the back of his neck. "Little one, you have so much to learn about control and who has it. You know you're not in charge here, know you're not topping me. It's not what Jesse wanted."

Tanner couldn't argue with that. Except... "I gave you your chance."

"And by agreeing to come here, you took a second chance. Same rules apply." Damon rubbed a large hand over the back of Tanner's neck now. "It'll be different. I promise."

Tanner wanted to believe him, but he couldn't. Not fully. But he was here, like a sitting goddamned duck. "Damon...I'm a top," he said for what seemed like the millionth time, realizing that all the times he'd said it he was really trying to convince himself.

"Jesse didn't think so."

"Jesse wanted me to comfort you."

Damon laughed. "Is that what you were doing when you were strapped down, spread wide and coming? Comforting me?"

Tanner didn't say anything.

"Impudent. Stubborn," Damon breathed, bit the side of his neck then replaced the sting with a soothe of a tongue. Pleasure and pain. "So now, tell me again what you don't want? Because right now, you're rubbing me like a bitch in heat."

Tanner's only answer was a low moan and his hand began to slip off Damon's neck.

"Let me guess. You fuck and you fuck and you're still never

satisfied. Can't get to that next level." Damon yanked down his jeans and then slid his hand down Tanner's crack, teasing him with the drag of a finger. And then, the gentle brush of fingertips against his hole.

A muffled groan and Tanner didn't bother to argue, was pretty sure only incoherent sounds would tumble out of his mouth if he opened it anyway. Indeed, he tried not to tremble as Damon swiftly pulled away from him, then placed a flat palm on Tanner's abs.

He heard a roaring in his ears, which muffled the harsh groan he was sure escaped from his lips.

When Damon's hand trailed lower, then lower still, he began to unravel swiftly.

"I'll come the second you touch my dick," he blurted out.

Damon smiled wickedly. "I know," was all he said as his hand slid around Tanner's cock.

Tanner felt like he'd be jerked off his feet by the force of his orgasm if Damon didn't have an arm wound around his lower back.

He slumped forward against Damon's chest, not bothering to hide his weakness.

"We're not done, my sweet boy. Not even close."

Tanner shouldn't like being called sweet boy, but he did. The term of endearment made his stomach flutter and his cock reharden simultaneously.

Damon was going to fuck him blind and Tanner was fighting both the feelings of arousal and panic that soared through him at those words.

Chapter Six

Tanner came all over himself, just like Damon wanted. He rubbed his hand in the slickness, then brought it up to his mouth and licked it off as Tanner watched him through heavy-lidded eyes.

The boy was still wary, as well he should be. Damon had never been gentle, but he was damned good. Tonight, Tanner would be his. He wasn't sure why that mattered so much, but it did.

"Bedroom. Now," he told Tanner, and the boy stumbled like a colt taking its first unsteady steps. He followed him, gazing on the hard muscles of the boy's back and ass, put his hands on Tanner's shoulders when the boy stopped next to the bed.

He kissed the back of Tanner's neck, then sucked, bit, sucked below the collar line, marking him.

"Yeah," Tanner said, his voice husky, the want and need overflowing. His hands were fisted. And his cock was still hard.

Damon turned him, eased him onto the bed on his back and began to lick him clean, starting with his abs and working his way down until he'd licked every last drop of come off Tanner. And Tanner watched him the whole time, his cock jutting between them, seeking attention Damon refused to give it.

"Damn, you taste good." Salty and sweet, like tequila and

salt and lemon. Tanner's face was a cross between desire and surprise. "Did you dream of me like this? Want me between your legs, licking you?"

Slowly, Tanner nodded. "The other night...before you found me...I couldn't stop thinking about you. Haven't been able to for sure since last night."

Damon gave him a quick grin. "That makes two of us, sweet boy."

"I'm not a boy...and I'm not sweet," Tanner ground out in a last-ditch effort to take back control.

But it was far too late for that. Tanner melted when Damon stroked his cock up and down, put his hand over Damon's as if to keep it there.

"Stroke yourself for me," Damon instructed him as he extricated his own hand. Tanner did so, slowly, as Damon played with his own cock for a few minutes, threw his head back and hissed as the pressure made his balls tighten.

When he looked back at Tanner, his strokes had quickened as he gazed at Damon.

He would have to make Tanner want it all, want it badly. Keeping him hot and bothered...all while he groveled just a little.

For a Dom like Damon, this was as close as it got.

"Hands and knees," he ordered. "Unless you want to go downstairs again... I'm sure there are a lot of men who'd love an encore."

That made Tanner blush...and made his cock jump too, and yes, his little boy liked to talk about being put on display, but not do the actual act, and Damon could work with that.

Tanner had gotten into the position Damon had ordered him to. He ran a hand along Tanner's back, felt the slight tremble...knew how much power this man had harnessed right now, kept couched...under control. "Gonna make this good for you, sweet boy. Gonna make all your fantasies come true. And you're going to tell me that you need it—want it—before the night is over."

His only answer was Tanner's hands fisting on the sheets and a small moan.

Damon had him on his hands and knees on the bed, still trembling, but spread with Damon behind him. Damon's hand on his back, stroking him like he was a racehorse that threatened to break his stall. He felt like that too, like he needed to stretch and run, but he forced himself to stay in the position Damon wanted. Tanner submitted—for Jesse. For Damon. And most of all, for himself.

Damon breathed against his ear, "When I saw you at the party, I wanted to strip you down and spread you just like this."

He knew he blushed at Damon's words. He buried his head in his hands and bit back a moan at the image.

"Would you have liked that, sweet boy?"

Damon ran a finger down his crack that made him shiver. It was like a jolt of electricity running through his core, and he nodded because he liked talking about it...liked Damon talking about it, but didn't want to actually be on display for anyone but Damon.

Then again, maybe Damon knew all of that already.

"Please." But Tanner didn't even know if he was asking, please yes or please no.

"Here you are, at my mercy...at the mercy of my hands. My tongue. My cock. So much to do to this ass...and I plan on taking my time."

"Yeah," he breathed. God, he was already barely able to form words and nothing had happened yet. The need to come was all-consuming.

Damon moved closer, as if mounting him. The blunt head of his cock rubbed Tanner's ass and he'd forgotten about breathing until Damon commanded him to do so.

And then he pushed back against Damon's cock without thinking, his body responding, doing what felt natural. Right. Damon's hands dug into his hips and Tanner felt the sticky precome getting him slick.

"I'm not taking you until you show your consent," Damon told him and Tanner knew the words would never leave his mouth willingly, no matter how badly his body wanted it to happen. But Damon had other ideas beyond words. Tanner recognized the heavy clank of handcuffs and his body went taut.

Would he let Damon take this all the way? Right now, his fingers flexed, his wrists were loose and nothing was stopping him from getting up and walking away from this.

Not until Damon dropped the cuffs on the bed, directly in Tanner's line of vision.

"You know what to do with those," Damon instructed.

Damon would make this his choice. Tanner could change his mind now...or strap himself down and do what Jesse wanted.

His lips were dry. He licked them, then saw Damon shove a bottle of Gatorade in front of him. He gulped it down and when Damon took the bottle, he wiped his mouth with the back of his hand.

And then he stared at the cuffs that seemed to mock him. Especially so when Damon climbed behind him and began to slide his cock along the crack of Tanner's ass, simulating what would happen once Tanner did restrain himself.

He nearly choked on a laugh. The thought of restraining himself willingly...letting himself be fucked willingly...

"You're meant to be fucked, boy. Trust me on that. Your ass is meant to be violated...taken any way I want. And I plan on putting my ten inches inside your virgin ass and filling you until you beg me to come. And you will. And then you'll beg me to do it again."

Precome dripped from his cock at Damon's words, and Damon's finger swirled the liquid over the head. "Yes, you want it."

Damon was breaching all his barriers—and he'd found them far too easily.

One finger slid inside of him, brushed his prostate and he jumped.

"You've done this to yourself, haven't you? Wondered what it would be like to have someone do it for you."

He groaned as the pleasure began to overtake him. Damon replaced his finger with a thumb...and then he pushed a second thumb inside. Tanner whimpered as Damon opened him, felt far more on display here than he had in the two public scenes they'd had together.

"Beautiful," Damon murmured and Tanner felt the puff of air against his hole. And he was ready to beg for Damon to just fucking touch him or maybe he did because then there was the slide of Damon's wet tongue along his ass, probing his hole.

No one had ever done this to him before. There was another wet rasp before Damon's tongue speared him, tongue and thumbs opening him, taking him, and he was aware that he was very close to incoherence. Opened his mouth but could only whimper, moan...and goddamn, it was amazing.

"The sweet boy's a rimming virgin too." Damon's tongue flicked the tight ring of muscle mercilessly, and then the thumbs left his ass to stroke Tanner's cock. One finger wrapped under so a knuckle rubbed the underside of his cock near the head, the other wrapped in a firm grip that encased him, stroking hard and steady.

"Damon, I'm going to..."

"Not right now."

Tanner followed the command without thinking—it felt as natural as breathing.

As the bed rocked with their movements, the cuffs moved closer to Tanner's hand, mocking him.

Three of Damon's fingers were in his ass, twisting, turning...scissoring. Damon's other hand was still around his cock. "That's it, my sweet boy. Fuck yourself on my hand, the way you'll be fucking yourself on my cock. Begging me to fill you."

"God...Damon." Right now, the two names were one and the same to Tanner. "Please."

"The magic word. But you still have to prove your decision."

Tanner fumbled with the cuffs, Damon never stopping his movements as Tanner put the leather-lined cuff on one wrist then threaded the longer chain through the headboard. When he clicked the second cuff into place, he nearly came.

The only things stopping him were Damon's fingers, firm on the base of his cock, not allowing the orgasm.

Damon chuckled softly, his breath hot on the back of Tanner's neck. "Good boy. Now, I'm going to show you your place."

And with that, the head of Damon's cock entered him...slowly easing into him, and he heard his sharp intake of breath.

"So tight..." Damon's voice was husky as he pushed forward, and the air escaped from Tanner's lungs. "Open for me."

"I don't think—"

"Don't think. Let me in."

It was as if Damon's commands made him forget about the pain, the fear, and his body simply responded, allowing Damon to enter him fully. His nerve endings were screaming but he remembered to breathe until his body accommodated the big man's cock. And then Damon moved, slowly at first, bumping his prostate, and Tanner felt the white-hot slash of pleasure flash through him.

"Fuck yourself on my cock," Damon said, stilling so the tension in Tanner's body made him taut as a wire. "Go on—you want to. You want to follow every order I give you."

A shudder overtook Tanner's entire body. He bit back a groan until Damon threaded his hands in his hair and yanked his head back slowly. Licked a line along his jaw. Bit his neck. "Do it."

Tanner couldn't hold out. He slammed his body back hard, saw stars as Damon's cock hit his prostate again and again.

"Take me," he heard himself say, his voice a hoarse command, his wrists stretched taut against their bonds and Damon paused for a second, rubbed the back of Tanner's neck.

"Good boy."

It all became a blur—his legs were spread and Damon was taking him, filling him, stretched him until he writhed like an animal, no control left.

"Yes, yes." He practically sobbed the words out. Damon took him harder now, the seduction having transcended its original purpose.

Boundaries...control...they were gone and he was left with the most primal need and well beyond logical thought.

He was an animal—Damon rutted him like one and Tanner wanted more of it—wanted it harder. Rougher. Lust slammed him—it was like hitting a brick wall at a hundred and ten miles per hour and coming out the victor, if not limping slightly.

Because yeah, Damon pounded him. He could barely hold onto the bed frame like Damon ordered him to do.

"Yes, Damon, don't stop, okay? Not now..."

Damon wasn't—everything was wet and hot and his dick spilled precome and he needed to touch it, stroke it. But he kept his hands where Damon wanted him to, and he moaned like a bitch in heat, the way Damon had promised and nothing else mattered except this. All of this.

And then, Tanner came harder than he ever had in his life, spilling thick ropes of come across the sheets and barely able to hold himself up. Damon came right after, his orgasm throbbing into him and Tanner wished there was no condom between them, wanted to feel the hot come inside of him.

Damon leaned down and breathed into Tanner's ear, "We're just getting started, sweet boy."

In the aftermath, Tanner's eyes blurred with tears he refused to let fall. Damon left his wrists bound together, but released them from the headboard so he could roll comfortably on his side. He did so, half-dazed, feeling sated and ready for more at the same time.

"I like keeping you bound and ready for me," Damon told him and Tanner swallowed hard, couldn't form the words...didn't know what the hell he wanted to say.

Damon looked at him with understanding and finally Tanner was able to speak. "How the hell did you know?"

Damon just smiled.

"Was it like that...with Jesse?"

"No. Jesse always knew what he was. You...so sure you were the top. Making yourself think that's all there was." Damon stroked Tanner's hair from his face. "You were making yourself goddamned miserable and you couldn't figure out why. I think Jesse knew that on some level."

"And you knew, right away."

"Yeah, I knew."

Damon hadn't been trying to humiliate him. No, it hadn't been about that at all, and Damon confirmed it when he told him, "You want someone to overwhelm you, to take control so you don't have to be so damned strong all the time. You're allowed to let your guard down, sweet boy. If I can give you that..."

If Damon could give him that...

And after tonight, then what?

Tanner refused to think on it, his body still strumming like an idling race car. The only thing he knew for sure was that he wasn't leaving the loft willingly tonight. And so he rubbed his body against Damon's, nuzzled his chest, licked and sucked on one of Damon's nipples as Damon continued to stroke his hair.

"You want more, sweet boy?"

"Yeah, I want more. I want to do that a thousand fucking times over."

Damon's laugh was a low rumble. "So you've forgiven me that easily."

Tanner pulled back.

"Hey, I wasn't saying there's anything wrong with that. You

91

should forgive me, but you've still got a hell of a big apology coming your way. Gonna make it so right for you. For Jesse."

"For Jesse," Tanner agreed around the lump that suddenly formed in his throat.

Kevin had been a patron of Crave, had consensual sex with two men inside the club and then walked out to go home and got taken without his consent, had a ripped-up ass and a concussion, and his life would never be the same.

LC rode with him in the ambulance, talked with the EMTs, hoped that Damon wouldn't find out about this before he could be the one to tell him.

Maybe Damon went home with Tanner after Rex's party. That would buy him some time before he had to tell Damon everything.

But first, he needed to hold a man's hand through a rape kit and a police report and the general humiliation that came with it.

The hospital was teeming with people—Sunday night, full moon and the ER was insane.

LC sat behind the closed curtain with Kevin, who wouldn't let go of his hand until the sedation worked and he calmed enough to talk with the police. This was long after the exam and the police's questions, and while LC sat there because Kevin needed him to be close, one of the detectives came over to him and asked, "Are you family?"

"No. I own the club near where he was attacked."

"I know." The detective eyed him a little warily and it took LC a moment to understand why. He'd seen the detective at Crave a few times, in much different clothing than the buttoned-up suit and tie he wore now. He guessed the man was hoping LC wouldn't say anything about that in front of his partner, who didn't look happy having to deal with a potential gay bashing.

Kevin's friends came in then and LC took leave of the small area to afford them some privacy. He stood outside in the cold air, smoking, wondering when the hell this would all go away.

The detective joined him shortly after that.

"You think this is a gay bashing?" The detective, who introduced himself as Paulo, but looked one hundred percent Irish, asked.

LC shook his head. "I think it's gay men targeting other gay men."

"You've seen something like this happen before at your club?"

"Not at Crave, no." But God, he'd seen it happen inside other clubs—so long ago he'd thought he'd sufficiently beaten the memory down. He fought the panic attack that could build so easily if he allowed himself to remember that night...and the aftermath.

"Do you think it's personal?" Paulo was asking, a hand on LC's arm as if he knew LC was unsteady.

LC jerked his arm away like he'd been burned. "I think all attacks are personal, detective."

"Point taken." Paulo took a few notes before speaking again. "How many others have there been?"

"This is the third. The other men didn't want it reported." LC met Paulo's gaze. The bright blue eyes boring into his held a heat that shocked his system. "I was handling it."

"You're going to have to tell your partner. The situation is escalating."

"I will. And I'll hire extra men," LC said tightly.

Paulo nodded, one corner of his mouth twitching. "One more question. Is Damon more than just your partner in the club?"

"No."

Paulo smiled outright. "That's good for me, then."

And it might be good for LC too, for one or two nights—if LC could handle the detective's touch without seeing another man's face instead of his.

The detective handed him a card with a cell number on it. "I'll be in touch. In the meantime, use the number anytime— personal use is fine."

LC went back inside and said goodbye to Kevin and then caught a cab back to the club. Renn had closed up and was waiting for him inside with the other bouncers, which LC appreciated.

"No press. No one seemed to know what was happening," Renn confirmed, and that was good. He didn't need this to turn into a media blitz.

"Where's Damon?"

"He came in around midnight. And then that guy, Tanner, joined him. Hasn't left yet," Renn said.

"Glad someone's having a good night," LC muttered, although he didn't begrudge Damon's time with Tanner. He'd been hoping the men would meet up at Rex's anyway.

The men were all circling around him, knowing they could easily catch LC's wrath, but he was too drained to go on a rampage.

"The attacker targeted the alley on the north side of the club this time, but the results are still the same—a man left beaten and raped with no witnesses—so where the fuck were all of you?"

"LC, we're really sorry. This is pissing us off too," Renn told his boss quietly. Renn had been bouncing at the club for four years now—was one of Crave's most trusted employees. The rest of the group might not care quite as much, but LC could see they were all visibly upset.

They damned well better be.

"If we can't keep our clientele safe, they will not come back here," LC emphasized, thinking about his and Damon's plans to shut the club down anyway. If this continued, it would happen sooner rather than later—there was no way Damon would let this continue to occur on his watch.

"We know, LC. We've got a plan in place. That's what we've been working on." Renn showed him the new schedule they would put in place for checking the private rooms, bathrooms and alleys on a rotating schedule.

"Good. I'll call in some extra help for the next few weeks. But I hope to hell it doesn't take that long to catch the bastard." And then he sent Renn and the other men home and locked up behind them.

The fact that this was happening around the club and living area of two former Army men was really pissing him off. Now, he would do something about it.

At the same time, the past was coming back to haunt them...and the third man, who should goddamned be here, was no doubt too far away to help.

LC went behind the bar to the small safe, pulled out the worn SIG he hadn't used since his military days and tucked it into the back of his jeans. Then he grabbed a full bottle of whiskey and a shot glass.

Tomorrow night, he'd use himself as bait. Tonight, he was all about remembering.

Knowing he'd be unable to sleep, he sat and made a list of men he could call in to patrol the alleys. And then he crumpled the paper and slumped in the booth and looked around at what he and Damon had created together.

Crave had been built at a time when both he and Damon needed something productive to do. They'd joined the military to escape years earlier, and once out, they'd come up with the concept for Crave as both a tribute to Greg and to their pasts. And even though BDSM wasn't LC's thing, it had most certainly become Damon's. His friend had been a great draw.

Styx had already been long gone by that point. Still was.

An hour before the attack, LC had been having a drink with a guy he'd thought about fucking but at the last minute backed away because he looked a little too much like that man from his past he'd been trying for years to forget.

So many things to forget...

It reminded LC that sometimes, there was danger inherent in forgetting.

A banging on the heavy steel door jolted them both. Tanner was still cuffed and Damon moved quickly, wouldn't leave Tanner bound for long when he wasn't there because he knew the boy would lose it.

He was still close to doing so now.

"Be right back," he told Tanner, who nodded.

It could only be LC, Damon knew, and that's what worried him most—his friend's timing might suck but there would be good reason for it. And when he pulled back the door and LC said, "We need to talk. There have been attacks outside the club," and then turned back away, Damon knew there wasn't time to argue.

He shut the door partway and went back to the bedroom, where Tanner was still hooked to the headboard, looking very well fucked. The boy's cheeks glowed, his mouth was swollen, and Damon ached not to be done with this yet even as he felt half-frozen from the look in LC's eyes.

LC was remembering that night and for the first time in a long time, Damon felt the chill go through him, had to hang onto the doorjamb until the feeling of panic stopped.

You're a goddamned fraud. Not strong at all.

His past shrouded him like a thick fog, the memories dense and painful, and he wondered why the hell it was hitting him like a ton of bricks, erasing all the good that had happened tonight.

An hour ago—hell, ten minutes ago—he'd felt like he was getting a second chance. He should've known better. The past was always with him...even when he was with Jesse.

Especially when he was with Jesse.

Getting close to someone...letting him in...that was a mistake. Because he could never tell anyone about that night—would never—and that would effectively destroy any chance of a relationship.

In fact, it had already done so and promised to do it a second time. He would stop it before it got to that—cut his losses.

"LC needs to talk to me," he said without further preface, ignored the unasked questions on Tanner's face as he undid the boy's cuffs.

Tanner shifted. "Right now?"

"Yeah." He paused. "I'll be a while."

"What am I supposed to do?" he asked.

"Whatever you want," was Damon's answer, the absolutely wrong fucking one too, but there was no taking it back.

"What the hell?"

"It's not like I cuddle." He paused, forced the words out of him. "It's what Jesse wanted—for one night only. You wanted that too. It's better neither of us get confused."

"You're giving me fucking whiplash" Tanner ground out the words, his teeth bared as if for a fight, but Damon didn't answer him. "If you want me to leave, tell me."

"You're a free man, Tanner—not my sub. The military would get in the way of us, no matter what." He threw on clothing as Tanner watched and walked out of the loft, down the stairs, leaving the boy confused and a little too vulnerable.

He called himself a bastard several times over for the man he'd left behind and the one in front of him who was obviously in trouble. Probably had been for a while and Damon had been too wrapped up in himself to notice.

LC was drinking whiskey, something he usually stayed far away from—and from all alcohol for the most part. And now, he was sitting alone in a booth, staring into space with a half-empty bottle in front of him.

He would have a hell of a hangover in the morning.

Damon slid in across from LC. "Tell me everything."

LC did. Told him what had been happening over the past two weeks, about the attacks. About going to the hospital with the third victim. "Tonight was number three. Same pattern. The police are involved since Kevin wanted to do a rape kit."

Damon felt the horror of the truth wash over him. LC filled and pushed a shot glass in his direction and Damon downed it, and then another.

It didn't help. "Why didn't you tell me?"

"You know why." LC didn't bother to say anything else—what was there? "This is the third one. I thought maybe they were isolated incidents."

"Obviously not." Damon's voice was hoarse with pain-filled memories he refused to let back in fully.

Judging by the look in LC's eyes, he had.

"The police don't even have a description. He hits them from the back," LC explained.

"One guy?" Damon asked, the shot glass squeezed in his palm.

LC eyed him steadily as the past flashed before both their eyes. "Yes. One."

"You don't think..." Damon trailed off and LC abandoned the shot glass for full-on slugging from the damned bottle.

"I think, Damon. I can't stop fucking thinking," he admitted when he finally came up for air and then took another swig. "I get that it's your pain..."

"No, it's not just mine." Damon ran a hand through his hair and let LC drink the pain away for the moment.

"It can't be the same guy, Damon—I think we both know that. Sixteen years would be a hell of a long time to hold a grudge."

Damon had. But he let LC keep talking, because the man had been dealing with this silently for weeks and it was Damon's fault he'd done so.

"Supposed to be a safe club. That was the point of this place—safety first. No one gets taken against their will."

Damon closed his eyes and still heard the clink of the chains...the screams...the begging. "It is, LC. We can't control everything."

"Says the great Dom—Damon Control-is-my-life Price."

"What did the police say?" he asked, ignoring LC's comment.

"The detective was hitting on me," LC slurred.

That made Damon grin a little. "Yeah, and?"

"And what? Nothing ever happens. You know that."

"It could."

LC just gave a short laugh and put the bottle down. "I'm going to hate myself in the morning."

Damon didn't bother to point out that LC seemed to hate himself every morning, even when he woke up sober. And he hated that he was powerless to do anything about that.

The only one who might be able to put LC back together was Styx, and Damon sure as hell wouldn't call that bastard and ask him for a damned thing.

Chapter Seven

It wasn't long before Damon got LC to bed. He lay down next to his friend, listening to him breathe, thinking about the way things were. The way they used to be.

On a night like this one, years earlier, with an icy rain pelting the ground, Damon lay sleeping with LC awake next to him. Back then, Damon had slept for three days straight, as if his mind refused to let him wake until his body had begun to heal.

He wasn't sure his mind ever did. He didn't dream of the attack that often anymore and wondered if that would change now. But being here, close to dawn, he didn't feel like anything had changed at all.

"What's happening is different, LC," he said into the darkness, and was surprised when LC mumbled, "You still get that same look, D. Brings you right back."

"I'm okay."

"Don't let it fuck with Tanner...with you."

Damon didn't answer him, because hell, it already had. He waited until LC began his deep, even breathing again and headed back to his loft. He wasn't surprised to find the door halfway open and the alarm at the bottom of the stairs turned off.

He'd practically pushed Tanner out the door. Couldn't have been more effective if he'd physically escorted the man out the door himself.

Tanner had no car here. The fear settled in Damon's throat then lodged itself in his heart until he felt his insides shredding from worry.

He doubted a cab would come to get Tanner in the middle of the ice storm—and unless he stole Damon's truck, the only way home for Tanner was on foot. Damon didn't doubt Tanner was stubborn enough to make it home like that.

He shoved a coat on and got into his Range Rover, heard the tires crunch on the ice that coated the driveway and finally found Tanner much farther along than he'd expected.

He must've left right after Damon went downstairs. He wore the sweatshirt and jeans and boots he'd had on when he got to Damon's, no doubt still damp from earlier and doing him no good in the storm.

He pulled up alongside of Tanner, opened the window. "Tanner, get in the damned truck."

Tanner had heard him coming—Damon could tell. But the boy was stubborn enough not to turn around, instead calling, "Fuck you," above the roar of the wind.

His lips were already tinged blue, but he was moving at a light jog.

"After you get into the car," Damon told him and Tanner gave him the finger and kept going. Finally, Damon pulled the truck across his path and got out.

Tanner's cheeks flushed and he cocked his head in a way that made Damon expect a right hook, at the least. But none came. "Why the hell are you doing this to me? I didn't fucking ask for this. I didn't want to lose Jesse any more than you did."

Damon didn't know what else to say except, "Get into the fucking car, now!"

"I don't owe you anything. I kept my part of the promise. I'm staying in the goddamned military and I'm not your fucking sub," Tanner shouted.

"Is that what you want?"

Tanner's mouth opened and closed, because he hadn't been expecting that. Damon hadn't either.

"I don't want to be your sub," Tanner said slowly. "But I didn't expect to want you the way I do, all right? I never wanted that."

When he'd thought that Tanner wasn't ready for him, he'd been damned wrong. He was the one who wasn't ready for Tanner...and he might never be.

When will you stop punishing yourself? LC would ask.

When hell freezes over, Damon had told him. And it looked like that might've just happened.

Tanner walked past Damon then and got into the passenger's seat of the truck. Damon followed, and they sat in silence for a long moment until Damon said, "It was my fault." Again. It would probably always be his fault.

"Just take me home."

"No."

Tanner muttered something through his shivering, punched the inside of the truck door lightly but didn't protest further. Damon wisely didn't say anything else as he let the truck's four-wheel drive grind them back to the club and the private garage.

"LC was in trouble—he needed me. And he's my family."

"What's wrong with him?"

"This has nothing to do with you...and everything. I should

103

never have left that quickly. Should've told you to stay in my bed and sleep and wait for me."

"But you didn't," Tanner said quietly.

"There have been some attacks at the club," Damon started. "LC's pretty upset about them. I've known him since I was fourteen. He was in pain." Damon got out of the truck and Tanner hesitated before following him. "Please, Tanner—I want you to come upstairs. I know you could've made it home. I didn't come after you only because of the storm."

No, it had been LC—the pain in his friend's voice reminding him not to let his past fuck with his future for the umpteenth time.

Tanner swallowed hard and yes, even this small bit of surrender was tough on him. It was tough on Damon as well, having to admit to all his wrongs, and dammit, he wasn't used to fucking up this much in the course of a week.

He put his hand on the small of Tanner's back and Tanner allowed himself to be led through the garage and to the stairs. When they got to the top and stood in front of the loft's door, Damon yanked Tanner's wet sweatshirt off first before shedding his own coat and shirt. And then he pulled handcuffs out of his pocket and clicked a cuff onto his wrist, the other to Tanner's.

"Why'd you really kick me out?" Tanner asked finally.

"You scare the shit out of me." Partial truth, which was hard enough.

Tanner didn't do anything for a long moment, and then he grinned and lifted their wrists. "These will keep you from being afraid?"

"They'll keep me from doing anything stupid." Damon walked into the loft and of course, Tanner had no choice but to follow. He walked right into the bedroom and tugged Tanner down onto the soft, warm bed, and they lay side by side, so

Damon could assess just how bad the damage was.

He knew there would be fallout from Tanner's first time. Just hadn't known he'd create half of it himself. And although he was still not sure he could do this, he had to make it better. Somehow. And so he covered Tanner with his own body and a blanket over them both to get him warm, and felt Tanner's body begin to melt against his.

He wanted to flip the man on his stomach and massage his back but the handcuff felt right around his wrist and so he settled for rubbing Tanner's lower back and shoulder and neck with his free hand. Tanner complied, letting Damon's hands smooth out the rough edges, accepting the apology of touch.

He wondered whether or not he was simply getting rusty from not being a practicing Dom or if Tanner was throwing him off his game.

He decided it was a bit of both. "I need to make sure you're okay with what happened," he said finally.

"I handcuffed myself, didn't I?" Tanner turned his head to stare at Damon, his eyes full of the memory.

"It was intense."

"Fuck, it was hot." Tanner paused. "How did you know...about what I'd like...about me?"

"I like knowing what turns you on."

"Is that part of the control thing?" Tanner asked without judgment and it caught Damon off guard.

Was it? Damon had wanted—fought—for control for so long that it was a part of him. It was who he was.

He'd been a part of the club scene since he was fourteen, fucking in back alleys and back rooms when he was supposed to remain in the kitchen washing glasses or mopping floors, because Greg wanted to keep him out of the main rooms. Greg, the man who'd taken him in and kept him safe during a time when nothing was—or should've been—safe.

But even so, Damon had a wild streak a mile long that wouldn't be contained, and once he discovered that he liked being in control, that older men liked to let him take it, there was really no stopping him.

He'd bottomed a few times, just to see what it felt like, and knew instantly it wasn't for him. He liked being the one giving the pleasure...realized early on that the man on the bottom held the control and the top just had the illusion.

That illusion made things so much damned hotter for Damon. Especially because most didn't realize the control they were wielding while Damon fucked them into the mattress.

"It's a part of the control thing," he told Tanner finally.

Tanner furrowed his brow a little and Damon could see the fierce warrior behind the handsome face, the determined soldier who would see things through till the end. "Do you ever get to lose control? I mean, I know what you said, that the bottom controls the show, but still...I lost control—I don't care what you say. When does that get to happen for you?"

"You worry too much about my needs, especially for someone who has no interest in being a sub."

"I didn't know you had to be a sub to give a shit."

Tanner pushed out of the bed and Damon braced for him to leave, but he didn't. Couldn't. The short chain of the cuffs strained between their wrists and Tanner stared at it, took a few deep breaths. Damon watched the hard muscles of his back move with the exertion, noted the new tension in his muscles.

"You don't need to be a sub to give a shit," Damon admitted, watched a bit of the tension drop from Tanner's shoulders.

"What the hell are we doing here like this?" Tanner wondered out loud. "It was supposed to be one night."

And it had morphed into something far more, nearly beyond Damon's own control. From the look of it, it was beyond Tanner's as well.

Damon talked him into sleeping for a while. God knew Tanner needed it and from the haunted look in Damon's eyes, so did he.

It was one of the main reasons he'd gotten into Damon's truck without more of a fight. Although he knew the Dom was highly trained, Tanner had age on his side, could've easily gotten out of that situation and walked himself home.

But dammit, Damon looked half-shattered, almost frantic, and no, that couldn't have all been from worrying about Tanner walking home in a storm.

Now, he opened his eyes and watched the man beside him sleep. Their wrists, bound together still, were stretched over their heads, each man lying on his arm, their fingertips touching and it was so close to being so fucking romantic and so fucked up at the same time.

He resisted the urge to stroke Damon's face, the light stubble on his cheeks giving him a wild, untamed look, more so than he normally held. He could see this man, belly down in the jungle, hunting, giving orders.

Fuck, it made him hot.

And then, he saw Damon jerk in his sleep, and he began to mumble—the beginnings of a bad dream that would continue if Tanner didn't stop it.

"No...just get the hell off me," Damon mumbled, and Tanner knew that wasn't meant for him. But the big man was getting restless, agitated…and there was something more going on here. Damon didn't seem the type to have nightmares because there were attacks outside his club, no matter how bad they were.

Maybe it tied in to LC. Whatever it was, Tanner wanted to stop Damon's pain the way the man had with him earlier. And so he slid down as far as he could without yanking on the cuffs, suckled Damon's nipple into a hard nub as he stroked his semi-erect cock, making it rock hard in his palm.

Slowly, Damon came out of the nightmare. Tanner felt Damon's free hand tighten in his hair, heard Damon breathe, "Yeah, that's it," and Tanner stroked faster. He latched on to Damon's other nipple, sucked hard, scraped it with his teeth and felt Damon jerk and release between them, the sticky wetness on his hand making him smile in the dark.

After Damon came, he and Tanner fell back to sleep until Tanner woke him.

"I've got to piss," Tanner mumbled, and yes, so did Damon, but that could wait. He was still sticky from Tanner's impromptu hand-job, although the boy didn't mention the dream he'd woken him up from.

Damon unhooked the cuffs from both of them and put them on the night table. Tanner stretched, headed to Damon's big black and white bathroom and relieved himself. Then Damon heard his steam shower go on. Damon didn't join him, although he wanted to. He did, however, watch him through the clear glass shower door, gazed as Tanner soaped his body and stood under the spray, his cock jutting into the air.

Tanner knew he was watching—had to—because he grabbed his cock and began to stroke, his head thrown back, his mouth pulled in a grin of obvious pleasure. Damon fought the urge to walk in and press his face to the glass, and he moved to stand in the doorway instead, unable to look away.

God, the boy was beautiful—tanned, strong, sure as hell of himself most of the time. What happened last night was the first step in making him that way all the time.

Except what was he supposed to do about the nightmares? If Tanner continued sleeping next to him, eventually, he would see a full-blown one.

Eventually, he would ask about them.

After Tanner came with a loud groan, spilling all over the floor of the shower, he leaned forward against the tile, the water sluicing down his back as he recovered.

"So fucking hot," Damon muttered under his breath, waited until Tanner finished and came out of the shower, rubbing his hair with a towel, his heavy cock and balls on display. "Nice show."

"Glad you enjoyed it."

"You'll pay for that later."

"Is that a promise or a threat?" he shot back.

"Get into the damned bed," he growled and Tanner didn't argue, crawled under the comforter and let Damon cuff his wrist to the heavy brass hook that flipped out from the headboard.

"Worried I'll leave?"

"Maybe I just like the way you look in handcuffs."

"Where are you going?"

"I've got to check on LC."

Tanner looked at his arm sleepily and then turned back into the pillow. "I'll be here," he murmured, letting the warm shower and the orgasm take him back to sleep.

"Damned straight you will be." Damon gave him one last look and almost jumped back into bed with him. But the boy needed rest—all parts of him—before Damon took him again.

His thoughts were confirmed by the ringing of the front doorbell. Who would be out in this crap, he wondered as he went downstairs to find a broad, tow-headed man in a black coat and pants standing there.

He should wear a sign that said detective, and indeed, the first thing he did was flash his badge when Damon looked at him through the glass top half of the door.

Damon unlocked the heavy steel door and let the man in.

The detective, who introduced himself as Paulo McMannus brushed the icy rain off his coat as he walked into the club. Damon hadn't been expecting him—neither had LC, from the look on his face when he padded into the main part of the club that his loft attached to, damp from the shower and looking like hell.

Paulo sure didn't seem to think so, judging by the way he looked him up and down, and Damon wondered if he should growl protectively or let Paulo have free rein.

"Rough night?" Paulo asked LC as he moved a couple of steps closer to the grumpy man.

LC just shrugged, glanced first at Paulo and then at Damon. "I wasn't expecting you."

"I was hoping you'd use my number first," Paulo said, and LC remained stoic, but a muscle in his jaw twitched, and as horrible as the situation was that had brought Paulo here in the first place, Damon was enjoying watching his friend being courted.

It had been a long time since LC had allowed it, even in this minor form. Normally, by now he would've told the guy to fuck off in no uncertain terms and continue saving himself for the ghost of a man who might never return.

"I just fucking woke up," LC said roughly, running his hands through his hair and shifting somewhat nervously. "Don't you sleep?"

"Not really. I spent some time outside last night, before the storm came in, looking for any evidence," Paulo explained. "I didn't find anything. I checked the databases to see if any crimes of this sort had been reported throughout the state and came up empty."

"Busy boy," LC said irritably and Paulo didn't miss a beat.

"After the storm's over, I'd like to go over the alleys a little more thoroughly. Talk with your staff," Paulo continued.

"The club's closed Monday anyway," Damon said as LC muttered something about coffee.

"If we need it closed for longer, we'll let you know. Right now, I need the names of all your employees so I'll have background information when I talk with them."

"I'll get it," LC said, stalked away into the office and slammed the door behind him.

Paulo gave a twisted half grin as he looked after him. "I guess he doesn't like to be asked out."

"No, he doesn't."

"Does that mean I should stop trying?"

"No, it doesn't."

LC came back out of the office, mug of coffee in hand, looking as pissed as before. He shoved the papers into Paulo's hand and went to brush by him.

"Hey, how about breakfast?"

"I'm not hungry."

"Ever?"

LC muttered a curse, glared at Damon and then Paulo. "Not a good time."

"It's probably the best time," Damon pointed out.

"We're in a state of emergency."

"I'm the police—I can get through. The diner around the corner's open," Paulo said, and LC looked like he was ready to argue. Instead, he turned around and went upstairs and came down a few minutes later, as Paulo was going over the list of employees with Damon. He had his coat in hand, boots on.

"Let's go."

"And he likes to give orders," Paulo said as he tucked the sheet inside his coat pocket. "I'm on this, Damon. I'm taking it very seriously."

"Good, because I am too." He ignored LC's final glare as he and Paulo disappeared into the icy rain and headed back upstairs. He put a lasagna LC had ordered into the oven, and he sat at the kitchen table and thought until he heard Tanner stirring from the bedroom.

He went in and unhooked the boy, who smiled sleepily as he stumbled to the bathroom. He came out to the kitchen a few minutes later, following the smell of the food, sat at the table and Damon served him a heaping portion of the pasta, with bread and salad and some wine.

Tanner eagerly dug in, as did Damon. He hadn't eaten all morning, his stomach in knots, but something about watching this boy...this man—in front of him, so thoroughly enjoying his food made him want to eat.

And do other things too, but hey, he had to let Tanner keep his strength up. And when both men were sated, they shared the comfortable silence and listened to the wind continue to howl outside, effectively stranding Tanner here until further notice.

He wondered what would happen when LC got back, how pissed he'd be at Damon for pushing him toward Paulo. But that's what family did, and LC was more his family than any blood relation.

"Where's your family?" Damon asked Tanner then.

Tanner shrugged. "They're around. In Manhattan."

"Do they know?"

"That I like to fuck men? Hell no."

"It's not easy living a lie."

"I'm not. I'm just not telling them a truth they can't handle." Tanner took a bite of bread. "Trust me—I wouldn't expose a girlfriend or a boyfriend to them. It's like a viper pit."

Damon stared at the man across from him and no, Tanner was too proud to hide. He was forced to remain quiet because of his job, but Damon always considered that a smart move for any man or woman in the workplace. There was no room for thinking about relationships when in battle. All that crap got in the way—made you weak.

The thought that he'd clouded Jesse's reaction times weighed on him heavily.

"Where'd you go?" Tanner asked when he came out of his reverie.

Damon didn't answer and the men ate in silence for a few minutes. And then he asked Tanner, "When did you know?"

"That I liked to fuck guys? Sometime in high school. I finally snuck out one night and went to a club downtown. It wasn't even close to being memorable. It was a blowjob in the back room, a fuck against the wall."

"And you knew."

Tanner nodded his agreement.

"And you picked the most homophobic institution to enter,"

Damon continued.

"Like you did."

"True."

"Look, I grew up rich. Really rich. Army was the family tradition. I'm supposed to serve, get out and go into the family business."

"Which is?"

"Investments. Boring as hell." Tanner drained his wine, the red staining his lips. Damon fought the urge to yank him forward and lick them.

"Will you do it?"

"No. But they don't know that." Tanner pushed some food around on his plate. "I want to stay in. I could make a career of the Army. At least that's how I feel now."

He met Damon's gaze. "It bothers you when I say shit like that. When I talk about the Army."

"Yes."

Tanner snorted at the one-word answer and Damon wondered how and why this boy managed to push all his buttons at the same time. He was angry and his cock was hard. "Snort at me again and you'll find yourself bent over the table."

Tanner's eyes flashed something...lust, maybe? And then he asked, "Is that a promise?"

Damon slammed the table to the side so he could get to his prey, enjoying the stunned look on Tanner's face. Had him up and turned facedown on the table before he could get his bearings. Heard the hitch in the boy's voice as he yanked down the sweats he'd put on him after he showered earlier.

"You like to push boundaries. See how far people let you go," he murmured as he slid a finger along the head of Tanner's cock. "It's going to get you in trouble one of these days...and today is one of those days."

"Jesus, Damon..."

"No begging. None. Or else you do not get what you want."

Tanner drew in a harsh breath but ultimately, he nodded his consent. Still half stunned by Damon throwing him over the table, and very, very naked, he knew he was at Damon's will. And judging by how his cock dripped precome, he was loving it, even if he'd be loath to admit it.

Damon's hand stroked his ass. "I'd love to tie you down and paddle you for this. But I think I know what would be more effective."

Tanner whimpered but he didn't say a word.

"It's time I pushed you," Damon told him, and knew Tanner wouldn't be able to help himself.

"You already did that," he muttered under his breath.

"Not enough, sweet boy."

"You gonna keep calling me that?"

"Yeah. And you're going to call yourself that too."

Another snort, despite his position, but that stopped when Damon reached down and spread Tanner's legs to put a leather cock ring on him and Tanner had no fucking clue where the man had gotten it, because it certainly hadn't been on the table when they'd been eating. But he didn't have time to think because Damon didn't stop there. Tanner felt the cold lube and Damon's finger rub his hole and then it was two fingers inside of him. Damon pushed and twisted and Tanner let the pleasure zing through him.

When Damon's fingers left him, they were replaced by something bigger. Knobbed. And vibrating.

"Oh, fuck."

Damon chuckled. "Yeah, that too. Now, tell me—say, 'I'm your sweet boy, Damon, and you can spread me any way you want me'."

Tanner didn't say a word and Damon increased the speed on the dildo, letting it hit Tanner's prostate, but the cock ring wouldn't allow his orgasm. Tanner grasped the sides of the table and groaned.

"So easy...you can come as soon as you say what you've wanted to."

And Tanner realized just how easy that could really be. His body wanted it—and the words spilled out of his mouth faster than he could stop himself, because he felt so goddamned safe here that nothing else mattered.

"I'm your sweet boy, Damon," Tanner gasped. "You can...spread me. Any way you want me. Any fucking way."

And he meant every word of it.

Damon unhooked the cock ring and Tanner came hard, cursing while Damon held him so he wouldn't fall off the table.

"Lesson learned," he mumbled.

"We're so not done." Damon took the dildo out, half lifted Tanner and moved him to the bedroom. Tanner didn't argue anymore, just lay splayed on his back, waiting.

And then Tanner said, "Come fuck me, Damon," and that was all the incentive Damon needed.

First, he held Tanner's hands above his head by his wrists as he kissed the boy along his shoulders and chest, alternately biting and licking the marks he made as he went.

Tanner writhed under each sting of pleasure, each lick of pain. Damon pulled back to stare at Tanner under him, his chest dappled with red marks and a thin sheen of sweat, breath coming quick, lips swollen from the earlier kissing and sucking.

"Beautiful," he murmured. "So fucking beautiful."

"Mmmm," Tanner mumbled as Damon's fingers found his hole, breached the tight ring of muscle and entered.

"You're still so tight...impossibly tight and hot," Damon murmured, and Damon added another finger and then another, watching Tanner move to fuck himself on them.

And when Damon used a knuckle to brush the spot that made Tanner jump, the man did just that, again and again.

But Tanner had made a promise not to beg and so far, he was sticking to it, despite the fact he was ready to come.

"Good...such a sweet boy," Damon crooned over him as his hand worked, Tanner's body rocking against his hand. "Sweet boy wants to come, right?"

Tanner nodded, his face set in lines of deep concentration—trying not to give in to the total pleasure.

"Turn over," Damon murmured, and Tanner did, hating the loss of contact of Damon's fingers. But he was quickly filled by Damon's cock pushing deep inside of him.

The punch of pain would always be there—that was part of the process. But the brush of the cock on his prostate made up for every damned thing. He hadn't known what he'd been missing.

What he'd needed.

"Come then, because I love watching you come."

Tanner didn't need to be told again, his cock erupting, pouring over Damon's hand, his chest, hitting Tanner's cheek. He cried out Damon's name, and then he closed his eyes as his body trembled, the way it did every time Damon mastered him in some way.

Chapter Eight

It was gray and cold and pretty damned deserted on the streets because all the smart people were staying inside. Which LC told Paulo, who just scoffed as he pulled the truck into the twenty-four-hour diner.

He followed the detective inside, wondering how to end all this personal-connection shit. Then again, he didn't want to spend the meal talking about the damned case.

He cursed Damon a million times in his mind and would do so to his friend's face when he got back to the club.

"What's LC short for?" Paulo asked after they'd settled into the booth, menus in front of them.

"My name," LC said, without taking his eyes from the menu.

Paulo snorted. "And everyone thinks Damon's the asshole."

"I definitely do," he muttered and that effectively shut down the conversation for the next few minutes.

But Paulo was a cop. Used to interrogation. Fortunately, LC had been taught to evade and escape such things.

"You're Irish and Italian. Your parents must've had a good fight about your name, huh?" he asked in a direct parody of Paulo's question.

Paulo just stared at him with those ice-blue eyes.

"Something like that."

"Cops don't like questions."

"Not just cops. Anyone who's trying to hide something," Paulo said, his tone mild, like he was enjoying the spar...especially because he knew he was winning, each of his statements zinging into LC as surely as if he had a target painted on his forehead.

He hated being this transparent. Usually, nobody gave a shit beyond letting themselves be fucked. Why did he have to find the one freakin' man who wanted more?

"I'm here, aren't I?" he asked with an exaggerated exasperation.

"Act like I'm holding you hostage a little more," Paulo said. "Although, maybe that's what you're into."

A sudden flash of Paulo holding him down, handcuffing him, fucking him, ran through LC's mind and his cock hardened in his jeans. He shifted and Paulo grinned like he knew and LC couldn't hate him any more than he did at that moment.

The waitress saved him from having to comment further.

"I didn't think you were into the scene," Paulo commented after they'd placed their order and the waitress, who looked exhausted herself, poured their coffee. It was some high-octane shit, and LC asked for a Coke instead. And he could've been a dick and asked what scene, but he was suddenly too tired to be that much of a dick. Until the caffeine kicked in, at least.

"Not really. Not like Damon."

"You've never, ah..."

"What? Been tied up like a hostage? Tied someone up and used my nightstick? Yeah, been there, bought the farm," he said and yep, dick-mode was back one hundred percent.

The eggs and pancakes came then, and LC just stared at Paulo.

"Must've been one hell of a breakup," Paulo commented as he soaked his pancakes with syrup, and it was LC's turn to snort. Surprisingly, he didn't feel nearly as sick as he should after all the alcohol. The water and aspirin Damon made him take before he went to bed must've helped, as did the orange juice and Gatorade Damon had left on his bedside.

Throwing up a couple of times to get all the poison out had worked as well.

Now, faced with food, his stomach actually rumbled, loud enough for Paulo to hear. Paulo, who was blonder than he was, a little shorter and built like a brick shithouse.

He dug into his eggs, ate for a few minutes before telling Paulo, "It was a long time ago."

"And you're still hanging on to it."

"Ah, fuck you."

"I'm hoping." Paulo sat back and appraised LC frankly. "I like you. I've watched you in the club for a while, but you never hang around long enough for me to talk to you. I don't like the circumstances that changed that, but I can't say I'm unhappy with the results. So let me help you forget."

"That never works."

"Then no one's doing you right."

"Look, I'm sure you're a nice-enough guy—"

"No. And if that's what you think—or want—you're shit out of luck, okay?"

"I'm not good for anyone right now," LC started.

"Yeah, see, that kind of line will only make the boys fall harder for you, trying to prove you wrong."

"Are you one of those boys?"

"I happen to be, yes. And I'll try as hard as I need to, because the thought of having you in one of those rooms...that's part of my nightly jack-off fantasy." Paulo had the nerve not to blush and LC felt his cheeks heat. Dammit. "You're getting shy with me now?"

Would Paulo tell him the fantasy if he didn't tell him to stop? Did LC really want to hear it?

Paulo's voice lowered a little, making the decision for LC. "You're wearing those jeans—the soft, dark ones with the black T-shirt and those black motorcycle boots that jangle when you walk. And you find me at the bar and you don't even ask—you just take me, right into one of the back rooms and then your dick's in my mouth, my ass...anywhere you want it. And then, when you come, and you're lying there, I turn the tables on you. Tie you down. Watch you struggle, because you realize what I'm going to do to you."

He heard himself draw in a low, stuttered breath and wondered if anyone would notice if he jacked off here, because now he had a new fantasy, one that didn't involve the all-consuming man from his past.

He chugged the Coke and willed his cock to go down.

"Why don't you come home with me for a little while," Paulo suggested. "I'll make sure you get back to Crave safe and sound."

That would be better. There was no way he was letting Paulo into the loft. No one stayed over—he did his fucking away from home, because he slept with too many ghosts already. "No promises."

"On what?" Paulo asked as he put down some bills on the table, refusing LC's offer of money.

"On anything at all."

Paulo lived on the third floor of a three-story private house—his apartment spanned the entire floor and was well furnished—minimal, but expensive. LC wondered how he afforded this on a detective's salary and decided he didn't care.

Instead, he turned when he reached the living room and pulled Paulo into his arms.

"Your terms, then?" Paulo asked with a cocky-as-hell smile.

"Always," LC murmured, brought his mouth down on Paulo's and kissed the shit out of him, as if he had something to prove.

What, he had no idea. Maybe that he could still do this without strings, without thinking about the man who haunted him.

Maybe this once, there wouldn't be a threesome in his bed. Paulo was more handsome than he'd originally let himself notice...the blond hair was a good contrast to olive skin and bright blue eyes.

Paulo didn't let him run the show—not completely. He was unzipping LC's jeans as LC stepped out of his boots and shed his shirt. Never one to put off getting naked, he shook his jeans off too. Stood in front of a fully clothed Paulo and watched himself appraised with frank appreciation by the younger detective.

"You going to take some of these off?" LC asked Paulo.

"Thought you might help me with that."

"I just want to fuck you into the mattress—if I'd known I'd have to seduce you—"

"What? You'd have left me at the diner?" Paulo challenged, reached out and began to stroke LC's dick, ensuring that he would definitely not be walking out of the apartment anytime soon.

"Clothes off," LC instructed and Paulo tilted his head but didn't follow the orders. "What's the problem?"

"You seem like a top...but maybe..."

"I'm a switch," LC said, his tone irritable, and why the hell did he offer up that information? He wouldn't be with this guy for longer than today, so Paulo would never get to see the switch. All LC wanted to do was flip Paulo and take him, good and hard. Told him so when he reached out and took his shirt off without bothering to unbutton it, leaving his tie on.

And then he stopped and stared at the swirls of color that ran along Paulo's chest and arms, full sleeves, and when he looked over Paulo's shoulder, he saw a full back piece as well.

A hot body and hotter tattoos and holy mother of God, the effect on his cock was more than instantaneous. And Paulo, the little shit, he knew, let LC strip his pants off as he caressed LC's balls.

"How's that?" he asked.

"Nice. Bedroom—now."

"How about right here?" Paulo asked, letting go of LC's cock and pressing himself into LC's body, right before he sank to his knees, letting LC get a good look at the tattoos along his shoulders and his back.

The scruff of his face scratched LC's thighs, and then Paulo was tonguing his cock, alternately licking and sucking until LC's balls were tight and he stopped the younger man.

"I don't want to come like this." He knelt next to Paulo and pushed him down to the rug, mounted him from the front even though he didn't always like the face-to-face contact. But this time...damn, he could barely think.

He only hoped he didn't call out the wrong name.

Concentrated on the man in front of him, the one watching him so fucking intently that he felt more naked than he possibly could be.

"LC...come on, I want to feel you come with me." Paulo's voice was part command, part plea but so fucking sexy that LC focused completely on him.

"Yeah, I'm here...coming now," he said with a calm he didn't feel as Paulo contracted around his cock, milking him to completion.

After ten minutes, he was up, rooting for his clothes. Until Paulo grabbed him and locked his body around Tanner's. "Stay for a while."

"I can't."

"Gotta go back and brood, right?"

"Asshole."

And so he stayed. Didn't want to go back and face Damon and their ghosts, and this was as good of an excuse as any. "What the hell's with your name?"

Paulo laughed. "Mom's from Italy, Dad's from Brooklyn—a New York City cop, like every guy in his family before that."

"Why'd you come here?"

"Needed a change."

He was lying, but LC didn't call him on it. "Any leads on the attacker?"

"None." Paulo paused. "Any chance he's targeting you or Damon specifically?"

"Always a chance, I guess." LC would not go there with Paulo. Not now...never. He stared at the ceiling Paulo had painted a light blue, like they were looking up at a clear blue sky on a summer's day. Simple, uncomplicated. Nothing like he was.

He was beginning to realize Paulo's ceiling was deceptive— there was nothing simple about the detective either, and he wasn't sure he'd be able to stick around and find out more. "Gotta run."

"Club's closed tonight."

"I can't have a life?"

"Not for the rest of today, no." Paulo tugged him down and kissed him in a way that made him forget about everything, including the possibility of leaving anytime soon.

Tanner had slept more intensely in the past twenty-four hours than he ever remembered sleeping in his life. He guessed Damon had been right about a lot of things, including the fact that he was meant to be topped, and he felt his cheeks still heat with that knowledge.

It wouldn't sit easily with him for a while, he suspected, but at least he wasn't scared of it any longer. Of his too-quickly growing feelings for Damon, yes, but at least he wasn't alone in that.

He rolled out of Damon's bed, saw the loft door was open and heard the arguing. Immediately, he headed downstairs in time to see Damon and LC toe-to-toe and wondered if he'd have to step between them.

"You didn't have any problem fucking him, though, right?" Damon was saying.

"That's none of your business, Damon. Besides, you acted like my pimp so you're surprised when I act like a whore?"

"You're not a whore, LC. For Christ's sake, and you accuse me of wearing a hair shirt."

"You had no right to push that shit on me," LC was telling

him.

"You had no right to keep this shit from me," Damon shouted back angrily. "This is my club too. I have a right to know what's going on."

"Of course you do," LC told him. "I didn't want you to have to deal with this shit. Sue me."

Tanner remained quiet, watched both men carefully. There was something far bigger going on here than just the attacks. Whether or not he would ever be—or should be—privy to it remained to be seen.

He was about to wait back upstairs, but then Damon stomped away from LC and went into the office, slamming the door behind him. LC stood there, looking angrier than he'd been before. "It's all right, Tanner," he said finally.

"I thought I was quieter than that," he admitted.

"Former Delta," LC explained. "You need to work on your stealth."

"Yeah, I need to work on a lot of things."

"You two have sex and drama written all over you," LC commented, motioned for Tanner to follow him into his loft, which was directly attached to the bar instead of upstairs, like Damon's. "He'll be in the office for a while. He's pissed."

Tanner sat on the couch, noted that LC kept the door open so they could both see the office door. LC handed him a soda and took one for himself, sat in the chair opposite the couch and balanced the can on his thigh.

"He told me about the attacks," Tanner said finally, and LC just nodded and Tanner knew he didn't have the whole story, for sure. Knew also that he wouldn't be getting the filled-in-blanks version today, for sure.

"How are things with you two?" LC asked instead.

"Better than they were the first night." Or the second. But still, "I don't know what's going on, really."

"Beginnings are never easy."

"I don't know if that's what this is. He and Jesse—they fit—they were into this whole scene. How am I supposed to compete with a ghost?"

"You don't know as much as you think. Has Damon said that?"

"He didn't have to. He's still in mourning for him."

"Let me tell you something, boy." LC's voice was sharp and severe and nothing like the way it had sounded the first night Tanner met him. "Damon and Jesse had issues before you were ever in the picture. And I swear, if you screw with him any more than you already have, I will hunt you down."

Tanner's brows rose. "I don't want to screw with him. I didn't mean to."

LC sat back and eyed him. "You might actually be the best thing that's ever happened to Damon. Are you going to get out of your own way?"

"But Jesse—"

"Forget Jesse," he said. "I said you might be the best thing for Damon. I didn't mention Jesse at all, because he wasn't. We just didn't want to admit it. He loved Jesse, but most of his mourning is wrapped up in guilt."

"Over what?"

LC shook his head and Tanner knew that if he wanted more, he'd have to go to Damon. For the first time, he did want more. From Damon, he wanted everything.

He was prepared to give everything back as well. "I can't leave the Army."

"I know that. Damon knows that. You just have to convince

him that he can handle it."

"Maybe he can't. What if this pushes him back to where he was after Jesse?"

LC shook his head. "No guarantees, boy. That's what makes life interesting as hell."

And then Damon was out of the office and coming toward LC's loft. Even though LC's back was to the door, he knew, rolled his eyes and muttered something under his breath like, *here we go.*

Damon entered and faced Tanner, said, "From now on, I don't want you coming here alone...or leaving alone."

Tanner snorted until he realized Damon was dead serious. "You do realize I can handle myself. I take out tangos all the time. I think I can handle one guy with an attitude problem. Maybe I can recon the area and wait—"

"No," Damon said sharply and Tanner just stared at him. "No," he repeated, more quietly. "Thanks for the offer, but I won't have you putting yourself in danger."

Damon was deadly serious and Tanner decided to let it go for now. He'd speak to LC about it, find out why Damon was so militantly dead set against letting him help.

"When you come, call me and I'll come out to get you," Damon said.

"You are fucking kidding me, right? I'm not a girl, Damon, and I stopped needing an escort around the time I started playing with explosives for a living."

"You couldn't take care of yourself the other night," Damon said.

"At the other club—that was different—I asked for it."

"No one asks to be taken against their will." Damon's voice was fierce. "You need to promise me."

No, he wasn't kidding, and LC remained quiet, simply watching the exchange. "Okay, Damon...fine. I promise."

There were so many damned promises growing between them, Tanner would be hard-pressed to pick them all apart.

Tanner followed Damon up the steps to his loft. Damon heard LC slam his own door shut and yeah, things would not be easy between them for the next few days.

"Why are you so pissed at LC?" Tanner asked.

"He's pissed at me because I made him have lunch with the detective who's investigating the attacks."

"Because?"

"Because the detective wants him."

"LC can't find his own dates?"

"He hasn't done more than fuck a guy here and there for a long time," Damon said irritably.

"Why's that?"

"He's mourning a ghost of a relationship. What else were you and LC talking about?" Damon asked, even though he had no real right to.

And still, Tanner answered. "You."

Damon bit back a smile and a curse as he watched Tanner sprawl out on the couch. "Any questions I can answer for myself?"

"Plenty, but I don't think you're nearly ready," Tanner said in all seriousness and part of Damon wanted to take the boy over his knee and spank him for that comment.

Actually, all of Damon did. "You've got a smart mouth on you."

"Always have." But he'd stopped smiling as he caught sight

of a picture of Damon and LC dressed in battle fatigues, cammy paint half off their faces. They were much younger, but their eyes told a different story—Tanner didn't know whether it was what they'd seen in the Army or before enlisting, but both had secrets. Too many. But Damon had his arm wrapped around LC's shoulders and LC was almost smiling.

"That was our first year. Taken right after boot camp." Damon remembered how hard the two of them had fought to make it. How they had more street fight in them than most of the other men, and that's what got them through the roughest time.

"I'm up for Delta training," Tanner said quietly. Damon clapped him on the shoulder, at once proud and sick to his stomach.

"You don't look happy."

"I've worked so hard for this...it's all I've wanted. The Army's always given me what I need. And now..." He shook his head.

"And it still can." He stroked the back of Tanner's neck. "It's about Jesse, right? Why you're having doubts."

Tanner nodded, looking miserable again. "I can't get it out of my mind...that night."

"If you want to know the truth, I can't stop thinking about it either. I want to know what Jesse said to you the night he died. I need to," Damon told him. "I've been going over it in my head for a year. Since we didn't leave things on the best of terms..."

Tanner blinked. "That's not the way Jesse made it sound. Well, no, he didn't say your relationship was perfect or anything, but he respected the hell out of you. Loved you. But he was insistent that I..."

That I'm exactly what you need.

He trailed off before revealing everything LC had been telling him about Damon.

"Was he in a lot of pain in the end?" Damon asked.

"I gave him all the morphine I had. I know it took the edge off—and that it also depressed his breathing but..." Tanner shook his head. "It was too fucking late. You have to believe that. His femoral artery was severed. I tried everything I could."

Damon was right next to him then. Tanner hadn't realized he'd started to cry and Damon was telling him he believed him.

"I keep thinking, maybe if I hadn't given him the morphine...he wouldn't have had trouble breathing...and he might've made it."

"How long after he was shot were you rescued?"

Tanner flicked a glance at him. "Ten hours."

"You and I both know he wouldn't have lasted, morphine or not. You made him comfortable and you gave him comfort by listening to him. By agreeing to his final wishes. A lot of men don't get anything close to that."

At that, Tanner turned to him, buried his face against the man's chest, and he let go, all the pain and anger and grief only allowed out for short bursts of time. That hadn't been enough.

He was vaguely aware of Damon carrying him, laying him down, curling up with him.

Damon's cheeks were wet too. Tanner reached out and wiped the moisture away with his fingertips first and then with soft kisses that trailed down his neck.

Damon's hand stroked his back as the men shifted, the dance rapidly moving from mourning to something far deeper.

There were no scenes or bonds, nothing, except the weight of Damon's body on him, spreading his legs, rubbing their cocks together...until Tanner realized he was never more happy to lose control in his entire life.

Tonight, there was nothing more between them than skin and promises.

"Yeah, please, fill me, Damon."

Damon let Tanner ride his fingers for a while, opening him. The need to take the boy, to help him, was overwhelming, and he hesitated, looking down at Tanner's face. His eyes were closed and his breathing was fast and Damon almost mounted him like this.

Almost.

Instead, he urged Tanner to flip, watched as the boy got onto his hands and knees, and then Damon slid his cock in with a long, strong stroke, pausing as Tanner dealt with the intrusion.

"So fucking big," Tanner panted.

"Flattery will get you everywhere." Damon felt Tanner contract around his cock, the man's channel so damned tight. "You're so hot around me, Tanner. Gonna take you so deeply...gonna make you scream my name."

"Yeah, please...now..."

Damon wished he could see Tanner's face, wanted to watch Tanner's eyes roll up into the back of his head as Damon went at him harder.

Would there be a day when he'd let Tanner wrap around him? That was an intimacy he hadn't even shared with Jesse, although Jesse never complained.

Damon had a feeling that, eventually, Tanner would.

Tanner, who was pushing back against him, clutching the sheets for dear life as Damon lost himself.

The nightmare caught Tanner by the throat and wouldn't let go. He was running out of the jungle...away from the gunfire and the shouts of the FARC soldiers...

Realized Jesse wasn't behind him any longer and doubled back, but it was too late.

Hands shook him, hard and fast, and he reached up wildly and hit and grabbed, and then he heard his name.

"Come on, Tanner...sweet boy...wake up. You're with me...you're safe."

Damon's voice, commanding him to wake up, and he opened his eyes and looked into Damon's dark ones.

"Make me forget," he told Damon, his voice hoarse. "Please."

Damon nodded, slid a hand around Tanner's cock and stroked until he grew hard. Tanner's skin was still damp with sweat, his feet twisted in the sheets below, and he moved with Damon, shutting out everything except the sound of the man's voice telling him to, just come, and then sleep...*that's all you need to do tonight—come and sleep.*

When he did come, the orgasm sucked the last of his remaining strength with it. He shuddered against Damon, felt the wet on his belly and thighs, on Damon's hand...a mess. A fucking mess, which was what he'd turned into tonight...every night he'd been with Damon.

But he didn't go back to sleep...because he actually hadn't meant to at all. Instead, he watched Damon clean him up with a warm cloth and tuck the covers back around him.

Three nights earlier, he never would've believed this could be happening.

"You still manage to make me feel like a man," he

133

murmured, unable to help himself.

Damon gave him a small smile. "You are a man. One of the best I've known, like Jesse."

"So I'm a lot like him?"

Damon's face softened. "In a way, yes. But in others, so different. I'm not looking for someone to replace Jesse—I could find a replacement sub today if I wanted—but the difference is that I wouldn't love them. I fell in love with Jesse, and I didn't think I was capable of falling in love with anyone. And fuck it all, I did."

Tanner wasn't sure what that meant for him—was it a warning that Damon didn't think he could fall in love again, or was Damon giving him hope?

And when the fuck did he turn into a girl?

He turned on his stomach, his face smashed into the pillow so Damon couldn't read his face, even as Damon's hand ran up and down his bare back. A comforting touch. A touch to keep him there, because Damon must've sensed he felt like running for the hills.

Tonight, Damon couldn't use the cuffs to make him stay because he couldn't. Had to get to post and check in. And he wasn't sure how to tell Damon, because that would break the fragile bond of trust growing between them.

Finally, he turned to see Damon's dark eyes boring into his. "You're thinking hard," the man observed.

"Sorry, yeah, it's just that...I have to head out so I can be ready for training at 0400."

Damon nodded and it was as if a switch clicked off. His hand came off Tanner's back, the moment shattered. Tanner peeled himself off the sheets and headed for the shower.

If he went home with Damon's scent on him, he'd have no

hope of getting any shuteye. And so he scrubbed up fast, realizing that he'd still smell like Damon's soap anyway.

There was no escaping the man.

Damon joined him a few moments later, enveloping Tanner's wet body against his own. Murmured something against Tanner's neck like *sorry*, or it could've been, *stay*...could've been anything at all and it didn't matter because Damon was okay again.

"I'll stay," he said.

"I'll get you up in time to make it to post," Damon promised. "I'll let you sleep."

"Sleep's overrated."

Chapter Nine

Crave had stayed closed for its usual Monday and Tuesday as well, partially because the detective had wanted it that way, and partially because the ice storm continued through Tuesday, an unusual occurrence that left the area flailing.

Now, Damon watched Tanner move through the Friday crowds on the floor. No one but the uninitiated would even attempt to touch him and even then, Tanner could most certainly take care of himself. And still, he hadn't done as Damon asked—hadn't been escorted in from the lot, and Damon remembered what it was like to be that free, that cocky, to feel like no one could touch you.

"He's leaving soon. Training for the next few weeks and then he'll move out," he told LC, who'd been sitting behind Damon's desk, helping him catch up on paperwork. Damon hadn't had his mind in the game this last week or so and, as always, LC was there to help pick up the slack.

LC, who'd saved him more than once.

"I know. Are you going to keep bitching that he's not following your orders?" LC asked.

Damon shrugged like it didn't matter, but they both knew that it damned well did.

"I don't know how to make it right anymore," he murmured.

"You made it right for Jesse for a long time," LC said. "Sometimes, a man's got to do that on his own."

Damon turned to look at him.

"Damon, I loved Jesse, you know that. But..."

Yes, *but*. Damon knew what LC would tell him, because it was nothing Damon hadn't told himself a hundred times over the last months with Jesse.

Your needs aren't being met.

He wasn't sure when it happened. Maybe it had always been like that, but Jesse's own needs had been so great and sprawling that they'd erased any gaping holes over their years as a couple.

"You put him back together, Damon. But if you're not happy..." LC had told him, time and again, listening patiently as Damon tried to voice what was wrong.

And when word of Jesse's death reached him, the guilt of what Damon had been planning devastated him.

The fact that Jesse knew about Damon's doubt made it that much worse. Damon knew as much as anyone that you didn't send a solider off to battle with too much on his mind.

He'd tried to make it right before Jesse moved out for his mission, made love to him the way Jesse liked...tied him up and gave him a night to remember.

But Jesse's journal told a different story. Jesse had known Damon was suffering.

I'm too selfish to give him up...I need him too badly.

"The past keeps getting in the way. Every time I try to move on, it catches up with me," he told LC.

"The past is in the past," LC said. "And yes, I realize the irony of me saying that. Do as I say and all that crap."

Tanner had forgotten it was Christmas Eve because he'd been so wrapped up in his training, in Damon, and since they started decorating stores in fucking August, he'd grown immune to all the red and white shit.

He'd never been the sentimental type and it wasn't like he'd be going home anyway, even if he did have the leave. So he wove through the club on his own, wondering how many of these men saw him the night Damon tied him down and put him on display. He'd come down here on the pretense of hanging out with the man, but he had more in mind. The attacks—and Damon's reaction to them—had bothered him for the better part of the last few days. He'd done some checking in the alleys on his own, which he wouldn't tell Damon about, and come up empty. He'd wanted to speak to LC alone about it all—the attacks and Damon—but that wasn't going to happen anytime soon, and walking around the main part of the club left him surrounded by a lot of men who wanted to get laid—and a lot of possible suspects.

He ended up at the bar so he could survey the scene, the burly man serving drinks pushing a shot of whiskey and a beer at him with a nod.

"On the house," he said and yeah, the staff knew him well enough as being with Damon. That thought made him hot as hell. A lot of men wanted to be owned by Damon, or so he'd heard from the murmurs around the floor as Damon did a walk-through.

He kept an eye on Damon, watching him stop and talk with other Doms. Did the shot of whiskey and nursed the beer.

He knew that Damon would be pissed that he'd come without an escort into the club, but did Damon even want him to come by?

When he'd left the other morning, there hadn't been much talk between them, especially because Tanner was distracted over the upcoming training. But he'd been to Jesse's grave the day before last, and he'd thought about what Damon had told him, that Jesse would never blame him. That he'd done everything he could to try to save him.

He wanted to believe Damon…was so close to healing and so damned worried about Damon, although he couldn't put his finger on why.

Now that he'd shown Damon his vulnerability, he wondered if he was supposed to feel weak or shy. Instead, he felt reborn. Between the fucking and the confession about Jesse, he'd gotten things out of his system that had been festering for too long.

When he started his Delta training yesterday, he felt like he finally had his goddamned shit together—and it showed. He'd flown through the first quals, and while he knew it would just get harder, the fire was lit.

The only thing now was getting Damon to commit to letting him balance both Damon and the Army.

It would be an uphill battle, but Tanner had a strong feeling he'd gotten under Damon's skin.

He finished his beer, watched Damon all but disappear with the tall man he'd been speaking with a few minutes earlier, and he wondered when the hell he'd gotten himself all turned around. He was about to get up and hunt Damon out when he heard, "See something you like?"

Not Damon, but definitely another Dom. Tanner looked at him but didn't answer.

"Boy, you shouldn't be looking me directly in the eye."

"I'm not your boy—or anyone's boy," Tanner growled. The man grinned, which made Tanner even angrier.

"I'll be the judge of that. And judging by your performance last week, you're fast on your way to becoming Damon's boy."

That bothered Tanner for more reasons than he cared to explain, and so he clamped his mouth shut and he walked away—attempted to, anyway. But the Dom's hand clamped on a shoulder and pulled him back.

"Boy, you need to learn some manners. I'm just the man to teach you."

Just when Tanner's fists were clenched hard enough he feared he could break his fingers and the Dom began telling him to not look him in the goddamned eyes and get on his knees, Damon came up from behind him, rescuing him once again.

"He doesn't need to be taught anything."

The other Dom tore his eyes from Tanner's and then left respectfully, with a simple nod in Damon's direction. Once he was out of earshot, Tanner said, "You don't have to fucking save me from everything. You can't."

"You weren't doing a great job of extricating yourself."

"I was trying to be respectful of your club," he explained. "I could've put that guy through the wall, something I also didn't want to do because I don't want to put my entire career in jeopardy."

Damon nodded and steered Tanner away from the crowded bar. "You shouldn't be down here. Because there are a lot of people who want to make you prove yourself. You attracted a lot of attention your first night here."

"Yeah, that was my wish," Tanner said.

Damon continued patiently. "You're not a sub and you're hanging out with me. A lot of guys would love to take what they perceive as mine. Show me up if my boy doesn't perform correctly."

The thought of being known as Damon's boy made Tanner's blood run hot this time. It was scary and a turn-on...and he'd never been more conflicted in his life. "Whatever."

"Go upstairs and wait for me. Because I don't want to see you down here with other men pawing you."

That stopped Tanner cold. "Wait. You're jealous."

Damon didn't answer but Tanner knew he was right.

"Would you like it if I was?" Damon asked.

"Yeah, I think so." Tanner paused. "I was jealous. I thought you were going off with someone before."

Tanner tucked his head in a way that Damon found so fucking endearing his throat tightened. As he'd walked through the club, he'd had more than one Dom ask about his new boy, if Damon would be collaring him...and even though he wouldn't want to make Tanner his sub, the thought of Tanner trusting him enough to allow Damon to collar him made his dick hard.

Although he knew the other Doms questioned his decision to back away from this world, Damon knew he didn't want his life to be a show any longer. He didn't want to put his boy on constant display—or any kind of display—and Tanner did not want that anyway.

No, Damon wanted private—and with his reputation and the subs that were constantly trying to get with him, it was seemingly impossible to run a club like this with any measure of comfort.

"Come with me," he said, his hand on the back of Tanner's neck, guiding him into the belly of the club, past the scenes that were happening right out in the open, play that was considered sick and wrong by some.

Once, Damon had lived in this world—lived and breathed for it. Today, he was grateful for what it gave him, but the man standing next to him could do more just lying next to him naked than the whips and the chains could.

Tanner was staring at the different types of play, first watching a young, collared boy at his master's feet. Another was being whipped on the St. Andrew's cross...moaning as his skin showed raised red welts.

Tanner's face showed his uncertainty.

"He'll wear those like his badge of honor," Damon told him.

"This is so damned intense...too much." Tanner turned away and Damon caught his chin in his hand. "You okay?"

"I don't know."

"You never have to do anything you don't want. That doesn't mean you don't trust me. Could mean you just don't like it. Could also mean you don't trust yourself."

"This place...it makes people feel safe, doesn't it?" Tanner asked.

"Most people, yes. At one time, it was what I needed. But LC and I are selling it now."

"Why?"

Damon opted for honesty. "I'm done with the scene. I was done with it before Jesse, but he needed it so badly. He liked the public humiliation aspect of it. The feeling of being owned."

"And you didn't like that?"

"I loved every second of doing it for him," Damon said softly. "But..."

"It goes back to what you want."

"Yes."

"You still haven't told me what that entails."

"I want someone who comes home to me every night." Damon hadn't meant for the words to come out roughly, but they did.

Tanner stared at him for a long moment and then he stuffed his hands into the pockets of his jeans. "I want that too, Damon. But it's not in the cards for me—not every night."

Damon understood. Could never ask him to leave a job he ultimately loved. One he was good at.

But Damon wasn't interested in being an Army wife.

"Do you want me to leave now?" Tanner asked him after a long moment.

"Yes. And no. It's going to hurt either way, Tanner."

"So don't fucking think about it tonight. Don't think about it at all. Let's ride it out and see where it takes us."

Damon wondered how he'd lost control of the upper hand in this relationship...wondered when it had become a relationship in the first place. "No thinking. Lots of fucking."

Tanner nodded in agreement and Damon tugged him in the direction of the loft.

Damon practically dragged him up the stairs to his loft, and Tanner allowed it, because he liked knowing he'd gotten to Damon.

He hadn't realized it before now, but Damon had more barriers than he did, and that was saying something.

"Get your clothes off," Damon growled, all while helping drag them off Tanner's body as if the need to reclaim him was all-encompassing. "Maybe I should've let that Dom have his way with you."

Tanner let a slow grin slide across his face as he threw his clothing to the floor and then palmed his dick, stroked it up and down while Damon watched him. "Yeah? Would you have watched?"

Damon sucked in a breath and stared up and down the length of Tanner's body as Tanner continued to jack off and talk to Damon, his voice husky with arousal. "Would you have let that guy strip me down? Bend me over? Because I think...at the last minute...you would've stepped in."

He threw his head back as his balls tightened.

"Bend over the back of the couch. Now."

He looked at Damon, felt lazy and horny as he moved to do what the man asked. He heard Damon's zipper, the fall of clothes and boots hitting the floor as his palms flattened on the cushions, his dick rubbing the soft leather. Damon came up behind him and kicked his thighs farther apart, fingered his hole with a cold slick of lube on a finger, the insistent press of a second joining it, twisting, opening Tanner up.

"Getting you ready to be nice and fucked. By me, not by anyone else in this goddamned place. Understand?" Damon smacked his ass once, twice and by the third time, Tanner was telling him that yes, he understood.

"Then say it."

"Fucked by you, Damon—no one else but you." Why was it so easy to let himself get into this headspace now? To bend over willingly, knowing Damon would be taking something from him he'd hung onto for so long...to be excited to give it to Damon again and again? "Please, Damon...only you."

Damon grunted as he slid his cock into Tanner in one long, devastatingly slow stroke. Tanner's mouth hung open as Damon kept him down with a hand on the small of his back and the pressure ceded to pleasure when Damon was up to his balls inside Tanner. "Gonna take you for a ride."

Tanner attempted to steady himself, but he could barely

144

hang onto the couch. Especially when Damon palmed his leaking cock and played with it in tandem with his own thrusting.

Damon had the strength, the prowess, but now that the fight was behind him, he needed to fuck through the victory.

He was like a rutting bull. And he was holding back—attempting to—and it sounded like it was killing him.

Doms didn't lose control, but Tanner wanted Damon—the man in him, not the Dom. Wanted to make him lose any and all sense he had.

Wanted to turn around and watch Damon take him...although this way was easier. So for now, he let it lie and instead contracted the muscles of his ass around Damon's cock, trapping it. He alternated that with thrusting back, hard, into Damon's hips. Fucking himself on Damon's cock, the way he'd been ordered to the other night.

Tonight, he did so without any urging from Damon, and when he looked back, he saw Damon's neck muscles stretched taut, his eyes fierce, his tone warning when he asked, "Topping from the bottom?"

In response, Tanner contracted his ass tightly around Damon's cock again and watched the man simply freeze. And then rut as Tanner squeezed again and again, milking the orgasm out of Damon.

Damon struggled not to let it happen and he failed, came with a howl of defeat, of pleasure, and Tanner felt the hot gush of come fill him. Reveled in it, his own dick still rock hard because he was so busy watching Damon unravel in fascination.

After the big man collapsed against him, Tanner wondered if Damon would somehow punish him by not allowing him to come.

"You little shit," Damon breathed in his ear. "Now I'll bet you want to come."

"Fuck, yeah."

Damon moved a few minutes later, yanking Tanner's head back by his hair to look down at him. Studying. Planning.

Tanner could probably come from the look in Damon's eyes alone. But he didn't, because he had a feeling he'd like Damon's other ways of making him come better.

"Stay there," he told Tanner, his voice gruff.

Tanner stood, felt Damon begin to rub the heated lube along the crack in his ass, then his dick and everything Damon touched began to tingle with a sensation that made it impossible for Tanner to stay still. "Jesus Christ, Damon…"

"Feel good?"

"Have to touch it."

"Not yet." Damon chuckled. "Little boys who get too big for their britches need to be punished."

"Please…"

"So damned impatient, sweet boy."

Tanner heard a chair being pulled. Turned to see Damon sitting, and he motioned to Tanner to come to him. "I want you to sit on me, baby. But first, play with yourself a little…make sure you're nice and open."

God, he was more than open enough, and the heated lube was making him nearly frantic. He played with his hole with his fingers while Damon watched, urged him on with a soft groan. And then, finally, when he closed his eyes and tried to make himself come by grabbing his cock and stroking, Damon stopped him. Turned him so he faced outward and then lowered him slowly onto Damon's rigid cock, impaling himself on the man who, when he was finally all the way down, held his hips firm so he couldn't escape and began to thrust upward.

Tanner squirmed, the pressure almost too intense for him to handle. But Damon put an arm around him to steady him and he let Damon do what he needed to.

"Fuck yourself on my cock," Damon said, stilling so the tension in Tanner's body made him taut as a wire. "Go on. You want to. You want to follow every order I give you."

A shudder overtook Tanner's body. He bit back a groan until Damon threaded his hands in his hair and pulled his head back slowly. Licked a line along his jaw. Bit his neck.

"Do it."

Tanner couldn't hold on for much longer. He moved his body up and down on Damon's cock—saw stars as Damon's thick, hard cock hit his prostate with each bump and grind...and then Tanner couldn't hold on. "Gotta come."

"No one's stopping you...never stop you," Damon told him, and Tanner closed his eyes and stroked his cock and came all over himself. And when he slumped forward, Damon held him. Picked him up after slowly sliding out of him and took him into the bedroom.

And Tanner wasn't sure what scared him more—how easy it was becoming to submit to this man, or the fact that he wanted to do it on a regular basis, even without being told.

Chapter Ten

Wrung out, Tanner lay half dazed against the sheets filled with come and sweat, and he didn't care about anything but how goddamned good he felt.

Damon was next to him on his back, his breathing slightly more in control than Tanner's.

"You staying?"

"Maybe."

Damon turned to him with a half grin. "Cocky. Stay here—I need to go back down to the club for a little while."

"I'll go with you."

"No. I want to keep you up here and away from all of that for now. You look so well fucked, and I don't plan on sharing any part of you."

Damon was so serious that Tanner's throat tightened. He wondered where this could go, given Damon's hatred of Tanner's Army career, and decided he didn't want to think about that tonight. No, he wanted to lay there smelling like Damon—marked by him—and he liked that he'd been all but ordered to remain in Damon's bed.

Damon came out of the shower, body and hair damp, strode around naked for a few minutes as he checked the security cameras, studying his domain before he slipped into his usual all-black attire.

Tanner's body went taut with lust. "You really have to go?"

"It's only for a few minutes."

"That's too fucking long," Tanner told him, loved the way the smile stole across Damon's lips. He jerked the covers off and strode over to Damon. "And I'm dirty."

"You are. You're my sweet, dirty boy," he told Tanner. He stroked his hair and Tanner fit against him, molded chest to chest, thigh to thigh...cock to cock...

"So fix it."

"But I like you dirty."

"Prove it."

Damon's eyes glowed. "You're getting in the way of my business."

"So punish me."

"I might. Maybe I will take you downstairs and strip you on the stage. Make you go over my lap in front of everyone, showing them all how much you like to be spanked."

Would Damon do that? He didn't think so—didn't want it— and yet Damon's words made him rock hard.

"Yes, you'd like that. So would the other Doms. Maybe they would each take a turn at your ass."

With Damon, safe, Tanner could easily give himself over to the fantasy. "What would you let them do to me?"

"I'd start by letting them tie you up. No, I think I'd rather be the one to hold you in place myself. I'd hold you from behind...spread you, let them take you, one by one. And you'd try to move, to get away, but they'd be fucking you so hard and you'd love it."

Tanner didn't mean to whimper, but he heard the sound

emerge and it made the look on Damon's face grow more intense and so he didn't try to hide the sounds.

"You'd like that, wouldn't you?" Damon asked as he nuzzled Tanner's neck, grabbed his arms and held them behind Tanner's back. "Would you do that for me, prove what a good, sweet boy you are?"

He opened his mouth to answer and something came out, not a word, but some sound that was raw and needy, and Jesus Christ, he craved this man like he was water in the hot desert. Trusted him, and Tanner never trusted anyone, unless it was his team on a mission.

This was no mission. This was...

This was quickly becoming everything.

LC pretended to stumble as he walked out into the back alley where the first attack had happened, lit a cigarette and waited. He hadn't told Renn or anyone else his plan, because he was pretty sure one of them was in on this. It was the only thing that made sense.

The attacks hadn't happened in the same place twice in a row, and LC's gut told him the man would circle back here looking for his next victim.

If it was JP coming back, it would leave LC little choice but to finish what Damon started all those years ago. When the club scene was new and fresh to both men. When LC had finally come to terms with the fact that Greg wasn't going to let him down, no matter how many chances he gave the man to do so. And he'd given him plenty of trouble.

"You're going to have to trust someone one of these days, Law," Greg would tell him, and even though he'd lived in the man's house for a year, LC had still avoided the human contact beyond nameless sex. He was fourteen at that point—too young to be doing what he was doing. Too young to know any better, but he felt so damned old.

Until Styx and then Damon came into the house to live, and he watched them interacting easily with Greg. Laughing, joking, even though neither of their lives had been a cakewalk until that point, either.

Those three men brought him back from a place so dark, he thought he'd never make it out. But Styx would come into his room without knocking, refusing to let LC kick him out, would whisper his name in the dark after LC would have yet another nightmare, would come in and hold him until he went back to sleep.

LC never told anyone Styx did that. Whether or not Greg or Damon knew, they didn't let on. But Styx finally brought LC out of his shell. Got him to sit at the dinner table with the others, like they were really a family.

Alone, in the cold, with those memories to keep him warm, LC realized this had been a big mistake. He hadn't allowed himself to think on the past this much in a long time, but with Damon wanting to sell the club, Jesse's death and now Tanner...well, things were changing, and he felt himself ache in ways he didn't think he ever would again.

Tanner and Damon were falling in goddamned love. As painful as it was to watch, he also hoped both men stopped fucking it up.

The back door of the club swung open, and LC turned swiftly in its direction in time to see Paulo, black leather jacket a startling contrast to his blondness, and looking very little like a cop.

Except for the handcuffs half stuffed in his pocket, but

everyone at Crave usually carried their own pair. "Hey."

"Hey." LC lit another cigarette and thought about quitting for the millionth time as he did so. Paulo joined him, took the cigarette from his mouth and took his own long drag before returning it to him.

"What are you doing out here all alone?" Paulo asked.

"Just getting some air."

"You wouldn't be trying to take down this perp on your own, right?"

He glanced at Paulo coolly. "I served in the fucking Army, you asshole. I'm not just some dumbass who owns a club and likes to fuck."

Paulo responded by pressing LC back against the wall and kissing him, hard enough that LC was startled into responding, even though he'd told himself that one night with Paulo was enough.

"And I'm not just some dumbass who can't see what you're trying to do."

"What's that?"

Paulo fingered the edge of the gun that stuck out of LC's side. "Pushing me away as hard as you can because you're scared."

LC laughed a little. "You're wrong about that."

"You're trying to forget someone and not succeeding." Paulo pressed both his words and his body against LC. "No, that's not true. You're scared you were succeeding. Because in my apartment, you came more times than I care to count and not once did I hear you calling out anyone else's name but mine."

Paulo's eyes glittered—half anger, half lust and all determination.

"I can't argue with that," LC said quietly, and for a long

moment that admission hung in the cold air between them.

Paulo's eyes softened. "I wanted to stop by and give you this." He handed LC an envelope, and LC slid it open and looked at the gift certificate to a local tattoo shop.

And he smiled.

"I noticed you liked mine and didn't have any of your own. Not something you want to rush, but I think you'd look damned fine with one," Paulo said.

LC stared down at it, couldn't look at Paulo. "Thanks."

"Glad you like it. I wish I could stay longer, because I swear to God, I'd let you fuck me right against this wall, but I'm working tonight."

This time, at the mention of fucking—and working—LC looked up. "So this was on the pretense of official business?"

"I plan to make you my business, any way you want it." With that, Paulo pushed away from LC and walked off down the alley. LC stood there with his back against the bricks, his erection straining his jeans, and he wondered how that man saw through him so easily.

Hell, maybe it wasn't that hard after all. He'd never been accused of being transparent with anyone but Styx. Every time he slept with another man, it felt like he was alternately trying to exorcise Styx from his mind while somehow betraying him all at once.

He pulled his cell phone out of his pocket, flipped it open and stared at the number that had been there forever.

He hadn't dialed it once in ten years.

Would he come if LC called? Had too much time and distance—too much of everything—passed?

There was only one way to find out. And so he speed-dialed the number and waited for the voice on the other end.

When the phone rang, Styx was alone in the motel room, waiting for Clint, aka Tomcat, to come by for his weekly check-in. Clint was now so deep undercover, Styx wondered sometimes if he'd ever come out of it.

Styx often wondered the same thing of himself, but tonight, he was all right. That is, until he glanced at the phone and his heart nearly stopped at the name that flashed across the screen. The name of the man he'd been thinking about as he fucked countless, faceless other men in an effort to forget.

Why now? It had been ten years. Ten years and four months to be exact, and he might be pathetic enough to know the number of days as well. Had something happened to the man he'd been unable to forget? To Damon?

With a hand that practically shook, he answered the phone and gave a tentative, "Hey."

"I wasn't sure you'd answer."

Styx sat up in bed, felt as if he'd hyperventilate. In a hoarse voice said, "For you, Law, always."

"I don't know why I called."

"Is everything all right?"

Law took a long time to answer and Styx just held the phone to his ear so he could hear his former lover's breathing. Took comfort in the fact that Law thought to call him at all, no matter the circumstance.

If he asks me to come to him, I will.

"Everything's fine here," Law said finally. "I just..."

"What?"

"Nothing. Started thinking about the old days. About Greg."

"Yeah. I think about him a lot myself." Greg would've kicked his ass from here to wherever the hell he'd been born for staying away from the man he loved for so long. For wasting time.

"I started thinking that I should've erased your number the second you left." Law's voice sounded hollow. "I wanted you to know, I'm doing it now. For my own sake. I have to."

Before Styx could say anything else, Law said, "Be well, Styx," and the line disconnected.

Law was finally going to give up on him. And while Styx was relieved as hell that Law might actually have a shot at staying safe, the hollowness inside his own chest threatened to crumble him.

Christmas Eve turned rapidly to Christmas Day. Damon had never really celebrated since Greg died—when he'd been alive, he'd always forced them to. At least they'd pretended to be forced, but Greg knew they all liked the presents and the tree and the dinner.

These days, he and LC celebrated by keeping the club open for those who didn't have a family. Christmas Eve was traditionally one of their busiest nights.

And Tanner hadn't gone home to his family even though he'd told Damon they'd been expecting him. No, Tanner had stayed in his bed, with Damon's dick in him for most of the time and let LC worry about the club.

God, how he looked, fresh, wet red marks on his chest, nipples reddened and taut from the abuse they'd taken from Damon's mouth, his hands...wrists bound and legs spread willingly. Heavy cock, still half-hard, despite the many hours of play.

"More, Damon. Please. I need...more..."

He did. Damon was glad the boy recognized his needs, because Damon definitely needed to give him more. Tanner was begging him to come and Damon would flip him, take him soon.

As much as he wanted to be face to face with the boy when he was inside him, he still hadn't been able to bring himself to do it. For him, that was the biggest intimacy, and he knew somewhere in his mind he thought that if he could keep himself from doing that, he could keep from getting hurt.

So far, it had worked only because Tanner hadn't pushed the issue. Seemed to like being taken from behind and held down, but Damon knew it was only a matter of time before things changed.

Tanner was changing. Getting stronger. Maybe so much so that he'd realize that he didn't need Damon.

Damon was beginning to realize that he'd needed someone like Tanner for a long damned time. Wanted to sleep next to him, wake up next to him. But first, the boy needed to come, and come hard. And so Damon turned him to his hands and knees and pushed inside and Tanner did come. Gasped, red-faced, tears in his eyes and a look of total and complete satisfaction on his face.

Damon did what any good Dom would do—held him for a few moments, gathered Tanner against him and just let him be.

"Are you staying tonight?"

"I want to, Damon. I just don't want you to freak out again and kick me out."

Damon studied him for a long moment before pulling handcuffs out. He used the now-familiar ritual, locking their wrists together.

Tanner stared down at the band of steel that connected

him to Damon.

"You like that, sweet boy?"

"Yes," he managed.

"Good." Damon pulled him close again. "I won't take it off, even if you beg me. Not until morning."

"That's probably the best Christmas present I've gotten in a hell of a long time."

Tanner meant it sincerely, and Damon understood. Between Tanner's non-relationship with his family and the Army, holiday celebrations were few and far between. "Me too."

Tanner smiled and then it faded. "I have more training this afternoon."

He said it quickly, like it was a confession he needed to share.

Damon nodded. The Army didn't stop for holidays. "From here on in, it's going to get intense as hell for you."

There was already some bruising along Tanner's chest, back and legs that Damon had noted last night and again this morning. His feet were ripped up from the long hikes and his hands were tough with calluses.

They would beat him down, the way they had in boot camp and again in Ranger school, but the Delta tests and training...that was something you couldn't ever prepare for. "You'll do okay. You've got the mental game down."

"I'm trying."

"You can't let what happened with Jesse fuck with you. You did nothing wrong. Everything right. Let it go."

Tanner nodded.

"I lost teammates, Tanner. It was hard as hell, and I swore my CO was made of stone when he told us to move the fuck on. But he wasn't doing it to be an asshole—he was doing it to save our lives. If your mind's somewhere else, it's not on your job."

The guilt of the fight he and Jesse had right before Jesse left for that last mission threatened to creep into the edges of his memories but he ruthlessly pushed it out again. This wasn't about Jesse or even about Damon.

Tonight, this was all about Tanner.

"Thanks for that, Damon. I know you don't like to talk about it."

"I'm trying."

"That's all I'm asking." Tanner kissed his neck softly, and within minutes, he was asleep, his warm breath soft against Damon's skin.

Damon slept as well, which was unusual and yet expected. Lying next to this boy for two nights had done more for him than...well, anything.

When he woke, he didn't want to analyze why. He just wanted to enjoy it, and so he brewed coffee and made breakfast and brought it to the bedroom.

Tanner was just waking up, stretching the covers half off his body...a hard-on, tousled hair and a smile. Damon put the tray down on the side table and knelt between Tanner's legs, heard the surprised gasp, the pleased moan as he suckled the velvet-skinned erection hard.

"Damon..." Tanner's voice was hoarse already from yelling last night...and Damon loved hearing that, knowing he was the one making this sweet boy crazy. "No one's ever done shit like this for me before."

"You deserve it." Damon ruffled his hair. "Let's call it my part of the war effort."

Chapter Eleven

LC was holed up in the office, planning the New Year's Eve party, going over the last-minute details as well as dealing with the real estate agent.

He'd come in here after the club closed the night before because he'd still been wired. Since he'd made the call to Styx, he'd felt uncharacteristically lighter. And unable to fucking sleep a wink.

So yeah, business as usual.

Now, the sun had come up long ago, and he was still bent over the computer, crunching numbers, fielding a few preliminary offers the real estate agent sent through. She'd done a soft perusal of the market, using word of mouth, and the numbers, despite the recession, were impressive.

It was prime real estate...great location and a built-in clientele for anyone who wanted to keep Crave the way it was.

He wondered what would happen to the place and then realized that he'd gotten sentimental somewhere along the way. Ridiculous. His Delta CO would've kicked the shit out of him for it, and he needed to do the same to himself.

And still, he reached into the desk drawer where he kept his files and pulled out the gift certificate Paulo had given him for the tattoo. Paulo had been working a lot but he'd left LC a message. There were none from Styx, although what the hell had he been expecting? He'd told the man that he was done with him.

The old Styx would've known that was total bullshit. This one probably did too, but he wasn't going to magically arrive and make everything right.

God, he was so fucking pathetic it wasn't even funny. And the fact the Paulo kept showing up in his dreams at the oddest times made the whole thing even weirder.

He was nearly facedown on the desk, his head swimming, when Damon came in, holding hot mugs of coffee. He slid one across the desk and LC grabbed it and took a long swallow.

Damon waited until LC almost drained his mug before asking, "Want to tell me what's going on?"

"No."

Damon sighed. "I'm going through hell here, LC."

LC knew it had been four days since Damon had seen or spoken with Tanner and holy crap, if this was what would happen after four days, what would happen when the time stretched to months? "Stop expecting me to pick you up and dust you off. I can't make everything all right all the goddamned time."

Damon strummed his fingers on the desk. "I realize that. Have you spoken with him?"

"Not everything is about him," LC challenged, and he could see that Damon itched to disagree, but the couched warning in LC's tone must've forced him to hold back. "You going to be in a shitty mood until Tanner comes back or until he retires? 'Cause I just want to know how long I need to walk on eggshells for."

"You never walk on eggshells around me," Damon pointed out.

"You're worried about him. Jealous as hell too. And you

can't stop thinking about him. Brother, do I really have to be the one to tell you what this means?"

"Don't say it, LC," Damon said tightly.

"Okay, but you're going to have to, eventually."

"Asshole."

"Yeah, that's why you come to me for the pep talks." LC paused. "I don't want to talk about Styx again."

"For how long?"

LC looked his friend right in the eye. "Never. And I hope that's goddamned long enough."

LC went over some of the real estate crap with him, even though he knew Damon wasn't paying attention. Finally, he told Damon to do this shit himself and stalked off to bed.

Damon didn't even bother to try, actually shut off the computer. Left alone, he brooded more, until he was sick of himself. Paced and wondered if he could handle another night at the damned club surrounded by willing subs and feeling more alone than he ever had.

For a long time, the club had been his refuge. Now, it was making him claustrophobic when he stepped inside.

LC had never been invested in the club beyond a business investment—this had really been Damon's heart and soul. Now, LC, as always, was simply behind Damon no matter what. If the club sold, LC would make as much profit as Damon, and he and Damon would decide what to do next together.

Even if things went further with Tanner, LC would always be in his life. The man couldn't be more his brother if they were blood related.

*If things went further with Tanner...*hadn't they gone far enough?

Christ, he was turning into a goddamned girl. And so he turned the computer back on and went over the comps so he could tell LC that he was helping.

When he heard the rumble of what could only be a customized bike a couple of hours later, he checked out the window. His cock hardened at the sight of Tanner on the big machine, knew how damned good the rattle of that vibration could get them both off.

He walked outside to greet the man. "What's going on?"

"Let's go for a ride." Tanner grinned. He wore sunglasses, a black leather jacket and his hair was wrapped in a blue bandanna that made his eyes glow. And no helmet. "We're going back roads," he said as if reading Damon's mind. "And we're going far."

Damon resisted the urge to grab Tanner and kiss him, but he knew that would delay the trip even more. "How long will we be gone for?" he asked, not wanting to leave LC alone for long, considering the fact that the attacker was still at large. But Paulo was still around a lot, no matter how hard LC was attempting to push him away, and that made Damon feel slightly better.

Tanner bit his bottom lip before he answered. "Couple of days. That okay?"

Damon ran a hand through his hair and thought for a second before deciding to stop thinking for the next couple of days. "I'll be right back."

He went inside and packed a small bag. Grabbed his own leather jacket, wrapped his hair in a similar fashion—black bandanna—and told LC that he'd be gone for the weekend.

"I'll hold down the fort," LC said with a small smile on his face.

"I don't mean to push all this shit on you."

"Just go."

Damon did. Walked to his own custom hog—a refurbished Harley next to Tanner's.

"Nice," Tanner said with a whistle.

"How'd you know I rode?"

"Just figured. Let's roll." Without further conversation, Damon got on his bike and followed Tanner through the quiet streets until they hit the back roads Tanner had mentioned.

They rode for about two hours of beautiful scenery and rolling, hilly roads with infrequent traffic, until Tanner pulled over at a lunch place, and he and Damon sat outside and ordered a ton of food.

The weather was unseasonably warm, which had melted all the ice from last week's storm, and Damon enjoyed the way the sun warmed his face. "How much longer?"

"Another half hour," Tanner said as the food was set down on the table. Both men dug in eagerly.

"You ever going to tell me where we're headed?"

"I thought we'd do a little fishing."

"Fishing?"

"Yep." Tanner grinned as he dragged a few fries through the ketchup. "And, you know, fucking."

That's what Damon was talking about. He took a bite of the lobster roll and wondered when the hell the last time he'd felt so carefree was.

He couldn't remember, but he was grateful for this. He tucked his feet around Tanner's legs under the table and continued to eat the food in front of him. And when they'd had their fill they got back on the bikes and pulled up to a private cabin in the late-afternoon sun.

"I rebuilt it myself over the years. It's a lot better on the inside than it looks," Tanner explained.

"Looks damned good to me." He glanced at Tanner. "How long have you owned this?"

"I bought it after my first year in the Army. Wanted a place like this to escape to whenever I felt like it." Tanner motioned to him. "Come on—I'll give you the grand tour."

The cabin was private as anything—the interior a mix of modern yet still managing to be rustic. Tanner had hit just the right balance. There were two bedrooms, one of which Tanner had turned into a small gym, the other held a king-sized bed and not much else.

The main room was a large living area and an open kitchen.

The cabinets were well stocked, as was the freezer, Tanner told him. He brought out a cooler bag from his bike and put fresh food in the fridge. Then they went outside to walk around the property.

"No one for miles," Damon commented after Tanner had showed him the lake and the various other trails and paths. Dusk would set in within the hour and they ended up back on the screened-in porch.

It was still warm, but the cold would settle back in after dark for sure.

"Yeah, I had the opportunity to buy the other lots and I figured I'd want the privacy." Tanner paused and then said, "You're the first person I've brought here. I like being alone."

"What changed?"

Tanner looked at Damon for a long moment before speaking. "You. You've changed me...in ways I never expected."

Damon wanted to tell him, "Right back at you," but his throat was suddenly tight. Instead, he cuffed a hand around the back of Tanner's neck and rubbed the warm skin as Tanner smiled. "I don't remember the last time I took a vacation."

Tanner rolled his eyes. "Big surprise there," he said. "Don't you know the saying, work hard, play hard?"

"Work and play have been combined for me for a long time. I guess that's not working out so well."

"No," Tanner agreed and then, without warning, he was stripping down. Damon's mouth practically watered at the sight of the younger man's pecs, abs and the deep indents above his hips that looked carved. It was a body fashioned by real-life work and not just a gym. Taut and strong. Bruised and battered. A survivor's body.

And his. At least for this weekend.

They had yet to discuss what happened when Tanner went back on Monday for more training and then away for a mission that could last a week or months, depending, mainly because Damon himself didn't know what to say about it.

"I think you should stay naked for the next forty-eight hours."

"I can do that," Tanner agreed. "But right now, it's time."

"For what?"

"Your interrogation." Tanner's tone sent a shiver up Damon's spine.

"Tanner," he started warningly, but Tanner was spreading out a towel on the porch and lay down on it, buck naked in the shade but completely exposed to anyone who happened by.

He really hoped the neighbors didn't have long-range telescopes, because they were about to get a hell of a show.

Tanner's cock jutted and he lay there and watched Damon watching him. And he laughed. "Come on. Clothes off. Get the fuck down here."

Damon did strip. If nothing else, he would show Tanner yet another lesson about who had control. And so he lay down next to Tanner and stared at the ceiling of the porch and somehow felt more relaxed than he had in a long time.

Until Tanner started in again. "How long were you in the Army? And Delta?"

Damon sighed, rolled on his side and propped on his elbow, looked down at Tanner. He'd play along for a few moments. "Altogether, ten years."

"You're going to make me pull teeth, aren't you?"

"Yes."

"Okay, but I play dirty." He rolled Damon to his back, moved down and buried his face against Damon's cock, nuzzling, licking.

Damon wondered if he should give the boy a warning, but his cock ended up in Tanner's mouth before he could stop it.

"Jesus."

Tanner played for a while, suckling along the sensitive skin before pulling back. "Why'd you get out of Delta?"

He gave the head a lick that made Damon jump and then he paused again.

"Bastard."

"Yeah," Tanner breathed.

"I'd had enough...saw too much."

Tanner's head dipped back down obediently. He was holding up his end of the bargain. Sucking, laving until Damon felt his balls tighten and then... "Family?"

Damon sighed, fisting his hands on the ground beside him instead of in Tanner's hair like he should be doing. "Fucking cocktease. And none."

Tanner shook his head as if to say, *not enough information.*

"Dammit, Tanner—you are pressing your luck."

But Tanner didn't seem worried, waited patiently, telling him, "I'm suffering too—my cock's so hard it's going to break through the porch floor."

Damon stared at Tanner's deep blue eyes. Guileless but not without intelligence and cunning. "I was put into foster care as a six-year-old. I don't know if you've ever heard of the six-year rule, but it certainly applied to me. I remained in and out of foster homes until I was twelve. Then I ran away, escaping that shitty existence." He looked to see if his confession was enough.

Tanner sucked one of his balls and then stopped. Damon growled a harsh warning, but Tanner remained stoic.

"I lived on the streets for a while. This gay guy took me in— no, not like that, Tanner—and he helped me. I was just starting to realize I enjoyed boys far more than girls. Greg never judged me. And when I was fifteen, I started working in clubs. Before that, I helped Greg out in the back of his, having to take cover when the place was raided. He was a club owner. He lived unconventionally, to say the least. Hell, I can't imagine CPS would look kindly on a forty-year-old gay man taking in gay boys. But it was never like that—not at all. He was aboveboard. Had his own lovers but never found anyone special before he died. Said it didn't matter, because he helped us."

"You and LC?"

"Yeah. One more guy too. He arrived around the same time I did," Damon said. "LC was already living at Greg's when I got there."

Greg's house—part refuge, part party and probably the best place for a gay boy to learn about becoming a gay man. He didn't have to close his eyes to remember how he'd felt that first day when Greg asked him if he'd like to move in.

"I have nowhere to go," Damon admitted, *feeling brash and a little more than irritated. "I can't pay you with money but I can pay you with—"*

Greg held up his hand and chuckled a little, although not unkindly. *"Son, you're not my type. I'm into bears, which you're not, and you're way too young."*

"You're taking me in out of the goodness of your heart?" Damon snapped.

"Something like that. I've watched you work—you do a good job. You come in on time, you don't shirk your responsibility and you're trustworthy. You're also going to get yourself unto a hell of a lot of trouble staying in that shithole motel."

Greg was right, of course. Damon had been itching to get out of that place and when he'd walked into Greg's home, a sprawling brownstone, he knew he'd come home.

He was pointed to the second floor and found his own room and bathroom. He had free rein of the house except for the third floor, where Greg's rooms were, although that rule would be tossed soon enough.

"You're not going to, like, force me to try to go to school or shit like that, are you?"

"I might." Greg slid dinner in front of him. *"But I'll let you get settled in before I start to mother the shit out of you."*

Greg had indeed mothered the shit out of all of them and they'd all grown to appreciate it. Welcome it.

Damn, he missed Greg. Greg would tell him what to do...help him through this confusion he felt with Tanner.

He was starting to really care about Tanner, way too much. And as much as he fought it, it wasn't going to work.

No matter what, Tanner was going to hurt him.

"Where is he now?" Tanner asked.

"He died of a heart attack when I was eighteen. He left us money and we invested it before we went into the military. When we got out, we had more than enough to be independent. It's what we always wanted."

The words poured out of him quickly. It was the first time he'd told anyone that story.

"So you opened Crave because of Greg?"

"Something like that."

"Jesse grew up in foster homes too," Tanner offered. "He talked about that a little. About you."

Jesse's background was eerily similar to Damon's in so many ways. He'd tugged at Damon's heartstrings as well as his cock.

"How long were you with Jesse?"

"We were together four and a half years," Damon said. From the beginning, it had been a push-and-pull tug-of-war, with Jesse needing more and more submission and Damon wanting to dominate him less and less. "He liked it when I performed with others."

"You Dommed other guys while he watched?"

Yes, Jesse was usually bound and gagged at the time. "It's what he wanted."

Tanner knew when not to push. "I've only had relationships with women," he confided. "Not exactly long-term—and not since I went into the Army, but there was something thrilling about dating a woman and fucking men at the same time."

"And you still like that?"

"No. Women aren't helping me anymore."

"Neither was fucking men," Damon noted and Tanner just snorted, neither denial nor admission. "I know you realize finally that submission doesn't mean you're weak."

"I knew that. Jesse was one of the strongest men I knew."

Damon stared at his cock. "You going to do something about that?"

Tanner shrugged and reached into his pocket to pull out a pair of handcuffs. "Put these on first and I'll think about it."

Damon stared at the cuffs in disbelief. Before he could get a word in, Tanner said, "Please." So plaintive. Strong. And as commanding as Damon had ever heard.

Tanner's *please* had been a couched, *do it now*. And Damon's cock had jumped in response, something Tanner hadn't failed to notice.

Damon clicked them on and Tanner simply stared at the way the silver cuffs looked on Damon's wrists as Damon surrendered by putting his hands over his head and waiting.

"So fucking hot," he breathed and Damon gave him a lazy smile.

"You've got the keys to the kingdom—for a little while. What are you going to do now, sweet boy?"

Fuck, there was so much he wanted to do, hadn't thought it all the way through, mainly because he knew Damon wouldn't let Tanner fuck him. Not now, anyway, although it was definitely something Tanner planned on revisiting in the future.

He moved up Damon's body and sucked on a nipple—hard, then bit below it, leaving a mark, his mark, on Damon's chest. And when Damon sucked in a breath, Tanner repeated it on the other nipple and then began to kiss a wet trail back down to the man's heavy, thick cock. Teased the big man with a suckle to the bundle of nerves just under the head and laughed when Damon's hips jumped.

"I might have to tie your legs too."

170

"Try it," Damon said through clenched teeth. Tanner knew full well that Damon could easily extricate himself from those cuffs if he wanted to. He made a mental note to ask Damon if they actually taught that during Delta training or if it was a trick Damon picked up in the BDSM clubs.

The fact that he hadn't, that he was playing along, well, that said it all to Tanner. Time to push his luck a little. With a few strokes to Damon's cock, he left it behind in favor of moving back up the man's body. He straddled Damon's face, watching carefully to see what the reaction would be.

When Damon licked his bottom lip slowly, Tanner let out a long slow breath. "Suck my cock, Damon."

He pushed his hand into Damon's hair, bringing his head up as though planning to force him. And Damon went with it, opened his mouth and took Tanner in, pausing at first to lick the crown and then stick his tongue inside the slit...and holy fuck, Tanner nearly jumped out of his skin.

He swore Damon chuckled around his cock then, because he'd taken it more than halfway into his mouth by that point, the warm, wet suck making Tanner pump his hips back and forth, fucking Damon's face.

Damon had sucked his cock before, but this...this was the fantasy Tanner couldn't get out of his mind...Damon, cuffed, helpless, submitting to him.

Damon swallowed him then, hummed while doing so, and Tanner went stiff and had to stop himself from coming.

He looked down at Damon, whose eyes never left him while his mouth worked, deep-throating him and then pulling back, the sucking sounds filling the air around them. And as much as he wanted to make this last forever, Damon was too damned good. The wicked glint in Damon's eye let Tanner know that Damon would make him come in about three seconds...and he would love it.

"Damon, Christ..." He gripped Damon's hair hard as he shot down the man's throat, saw stars and managed to pull himself back so he wasn't choking Damon.

Damon seemed none the worse for wear, just licked his lips in an obscene manner that made Tanner want to do it all over again.

Damon remained on his back on the porch, wrists cuffed and his cock hard as hell. And he was actually fucking okay with it.

And once Tanner could move again, Tanner guided him up, still cuffed, and brought him inside into the bedroom.

"You don't have to do anything. Just lie down," Tanner instructed.

Damon found himself obeying. And liking it, although this wasn't close to D/s. No, this was Tanner's way of making him relax. But the switch was palpable. Damon hadn't realized he'd been falling into old patterns until Tanner shoved him out of them—roughly. By necessity.

Taking care of him like no one ever had before.

"Come here," he said huskily. This time, Tanner complied easily, lying on the bed beside him. "I know I don't have to do anything...but I want to. So take these off and put them on yourself for me."

Tanner's face flushed. "I need to finish what I started with you." Even as he spoke, his hand went between Damon's legs. "I'm not a cocktease."

"No, you're not, baby. But getting you off gets me off, so let me."

Tanner looked unsure, but he did as Damon asked. Damon

grabbed the boy then, swung him so Tanner was on his back with Damon over him. "That was really goddamned hot, Tanner."

"Yeah."

He stroked down the side of Tanner's face. "Put the cuffs on."

He got off the bed and rummaged through his bag, hearing the click as Tanner complied with the request. When he came back, he was holding a leather cock ring that he promptly snapped on at the base of Tanner's cock, snugly.

Tanner just stared at it.

"Can't come without my help this time for sure." Damon smirked. "On your hands and knees, the way I like you."

Tanner swallowed hard, hesitated only for a second before doing so. Once splayed there, Damon simply buried his face in Tanner's ass, sucking, licking, spearing his tongue so he could fuck the boy that way.

"Damon...Damon..." Tanner just repeated his name, over and over as his body began to tremble. Damon knew how hard it was for Tanner to not collapse downward—to have his cock hanging in the air without a touch to stop the intense pressure—and so Damon reached forward and stroked the already hard cock.

Pure, sweet torture for the boy, and Damon enjoyed every second of giving it. Licked and sucked and stroked until Tanner went down on his elbows, whimpering, sweating.

It was only then Damon released the leather cock ring, allowing Tanner to explode against his chest, the sheets...shuddering, cursing and moaning all at once.

Damon's legs stretched, his toes curled and he came hard against the sheets with his face still buried in Tanner's ass.

When he was able to move, he crawled up to Tanner, who took one look at his come-soaked chest and stomach and leaned in to lap it up, licking and cleaning.

Damon watched, his dick growing more than half-hard almost instantly as Tanner's tongue rasped against his cock now, cleaning the head.

"Nice job, baby boy. God, you're good."

And when Tanner finished, he curled up next to Damon.

Damon turned into him, rubbed his back. "Are you okay?"

"You have to ask?"

"Always."

Tanner shifted and propped his head up on his arm. "We're not in a scene, you know."

"Scene or not, I'm always going to make sure I didn't press your limits too far, too fast."

Tanner nodded. "You didn't. Did I push yours?"

The little shit had, but Damon would be damned if he admitted it. Instead, he rolled off the bed with a derisive snort and headed to the shower.

Under the hot spray, with the steam shower pumping, he braced his palms against the wall and ducked his head, letting the water wash over his head and pound the back of his neck.

Thinking too much—should be fucking, not thinking.

He would make sure the rest of the weekend went that way.

Chapter Twelve

Damon came inside after a long afternoon of lying in a hammock doing absolutely nothing—and enjoying that for the first time in forever.

He found Tanner wasn't nearly as content. He'd gone fishing for a while that afternoon and was supposed to join Damon outside after he'd put his gear away. When that didn't happen, Damon went looking for the boy and found him sitting on the couch staring into space.

Anger radiated off him in waves, and he spoke before Damon had the chance to.

"I'm re-upping," he said, his voice harsh, like he expected an argument. He hadn't discussed it with Damon yet—not that he had to, and still, it made Damon's stomach tighten.

Tanner held his cell phone in his hand. "I just told my family the good news."

"You called them?"

He nodded. "My mother—trying to talk me out of it. She called to check in, to make sure that I was still on track to get out and join the family. Then my father told me that I'd forfeit my trust if I stayed enlisted."

"What did you say?"

"I told them to send me the papers and I'll sign off on all

rights to my inheritance. I don't want it—never did." Tanner's voice was rough with truth and with the pain of losing his family. "There's no repairing the relationship between us. If they can't handle me in the Army, they sure as hell couldn't handle me being in a relationship with a guy."

"Is that what this is?" Damon asked, then wished he hadn't.

"Ah, fuck, Damon, don't start that shit with me." He threw the phone to the table and slammed into the next room where he'd converted a bedroom into a gym.

The man was always working out—for special forces, Rangers, you had to in order to be in top shape—but it was obvious Tanner was training harder these days.

He'd gone out for a run that morning—Damon had watched him leave the cabin as the dawn approached. Now, Damon waited for a little while, listening to the heavy clank of the equipment before he walked in.

Tanner had stripped down to a black wifebeater and baggy Nike shorts. His feet were bare as he worked the heavy weights, his muscles bunching as he curled the heavy dumbbells toward his chest. His body was covered with a fine sheen of sweat, and Damon couldn't help but stare at the fine specimen Tanner was...forgetting for just a moment that he was pissed as hell at Tanner for breaking his re-upping news to him that way.

The boy could do whatever he liked, but he knew it was a problem for Damon, that it always would be.

And yet, there were bigger issues between them than that. "How much money are you giving up?" he asked finally, and Tanner let the weights drop to the floor with a loud clang.

"Does it really matter?" he asked. "A lot. Enough to keep me for the rest of my life."

Damon nodded as he watched the sun setting through the

bay window behind the couch. Their last night here, before they got on their bikes and headed back to the reality that had already begun to poke its unwanted head in. "And you're sure—"

"Yes." Tanner didn't give him any more room to ask questions. "Are you going to fuck me now or what?"

"Well, when you ask me as nicely as that." Damon could feel the anger radiating from the boy. Although calm in his decision, talking with Damon had angered Tanner almost to the point of no return. Even with the workout, the tension in his muscles was noticeable.

Damon would need to remedy that. "Get on your hands and knees."

"Going all Dom on me, are you?" Tanner cocked a brow and remained sitting.

"Don't press your luck—you know I can take you out of that chair and down on the floor."

Tanner didn't move for a long moment and then, with just a trace of hesitation, did what Damon asked.

Still, he was anything but cooperative—the snarling look on his face told him Tanner was not prepared to do what Damon said.

Damon always did like a challenge. It was time to do what he did best...time to finally break through Tanner's barriers for good. And he left Tanner there for a long moment while he went to his bag to retrieve the handcuffs and took his time getting back to the room.

"Am I in a time-out?" Tanner asked.

"You're going to wish you were," Damon told him, bent down and showed Tanner the cuffs.

Tanner fought them this time, told Damon, "Forget it," but

Damon wouldn't let him make that choice. No, just like Damon had told him, Tanner needed someone to take the choice from him.

"Damon, I said no—not now."

"Don't make me gag you."

Tanner gave a *yeah right* snort and Damon slapped his ass, hard enough to make the boy jump.

"Done being a smartass?"

When Tanner didn't answer, he knew they were part of the way there. And he cuffed Tanner's wrists, wrapping the chain around a bar of the heavy machinery, which would allow Tanner to tall kneel but nothing more.

There was no way for Tanner to free himself—the machine had been bolted to the floor.

There was no chance of escape, and Tanner finally saw that.

"Please, Damon," he started.

"Yeah, the nice act's not going to get you shit."

"Neither is subbing."

"Trust me, this doesn't make you my sub. But you need this, more than you know." He bent and pulled Tanner's shorts off, stroked Tanner's half-hard dick with a rough touch as he inhaled the musky smell of sweat and man. And then he bit Tanner on the back of the neck and heard the boy gasp.

Pleasure and pain, and Tanner would have all of it now.

"Turns you on to have all the power, doesn't it?" Tanner spit out.

"Everything about you turns me the fuck on," Damon told him. "You don't know how badly I wanted to fuck you that first night. Watching you bent over...chained down...fighting it and still wanting it anyway."

Tanner's breathing was harsh as Damon brought him back to their first night together.

"And they were all watching you. Wondering how I got so damned lucky to have you under me."

"And you didn't have me." Tanner's voice was a growl.

"Still mad at me about that."

Tanner groaned under the touch but his body was tense.

"You think I rejected you just like your family did? That nothing I've done since then has really made up for it?"

Tanner came then, reluctantly, because Damon dragged the orgasm from him. And Damon didn't wait. He entered him, since he'd slicked himself while he was speaking with Tanner...

"Fuck..."

"Exactly." Damon rode him the way he'd wanted to...the way Tanner wanted him to. "This is what you wanted, wanted me to take it from you that night so you wouldn't have to explain it or talk about it or deal with it. So you could say you tried it and could go back to topping and fucking everyone in sight...and you'd still end up so damned unfulfilled you'd wonder what the hell was wrong with you.'

With that, he bucked against Tanner, buried to the hilt inside his ass so Tanner was alternately trying to get fucked harder and trying to get away from the intensity.

It was only after they both came to screaming orgasms that Damon bent his head and finished his thought, whispering directly into Tanner's ear, "There's nothing wrong with you, boy...you're fucking perfect."

And when Tanner started to sob, Damon knew he'd gotten through. He'd finally, for fucking sure, gotten through.

Just as quickly as the vacation had begun, it was over. The ride home was uneventful—both men on their own bikes, leaving the cabin behind them...but they'd both still come away with something from the trip they'd never expected.

And although Tanner was far more at peace with himself than when they'd started the trip, Damon was getting farther from it. Maybe because he knew there was no chance of getting Tanner to stay with him tonight, because the man needed to check into post within the next few hours.

When they arrived at Crave, Tanner parked his bike out front, prepared to follow Damon to the club, as if protecting him.

"I don't need an escort."

"I think you do," Tanner told him with a grin and Damon grunted and got off his bike.

"You're lucky I like you, or else I'd kick your ass."

"You've been doing that already." Tanner's face flushed a little but the smile didn't leave his eyes. "You going to be able to do this? You and me—giving it a try? Because I'm re-upping. I'm not reconsidering that."

Was he? "I'm still here."

"That's a good start." The smile spread across the sweet boy's face. "A damned fine start."

It was. And still, "Look, if this is about being independent...I have money. You don't need to worry about your family cutting you off."

"It's not about the money, Damon. I think you know that."

He did. Stroked Tanner's cheek and wished to hell he didn't know. Didn't want to think about him getting hurt.

"I could get hurt crossing the street," Tanner said, reading Damon's mind, which wasn't that hard to do right now at all.

"That's what the recruiters tell the nervous mamas. It never worked on them either," Damon said quietly, knowing full well that tomorrow, Tanner started training for a new mission, which meant he was certain to move out to the real thing sooner rather than later.

He also realized, with a certain sense of irony, that by helping Tanner rid himself of his guilt over Jesse's death, he'd paved the way for the man to enter the even more dangerous world of Delta Force. In effect, he'd helped Tanner stay in the Army.

"I want to come home to you. Do you understand that?" Tanner asked fiercely, grabbing Damon's face in his hands. "I never had that before. I'm not losing you when I just found you."

"You don't have control over that."

"Neither do you. Not even if you locked me in the club," Tanner pointed out and Damon didn't know what to say. His throat tightened. "Just don't give up on me, Damon. Please."

He wanted to say he wouldn't, but the words wouldn't come out. Tanner didn't force the issue, just dropped his hands from Damon's face and revved up his bike. And then he rode away, leaving the ball entirely in Damon's court.

Chapter Thirteen

Damon made it through New Year's Eve at the club and the week after, all without hearing a word from Tanner. He'd almost convinced himself that he could do this, because the attacks had seemingly come to a halt with the presence of extra security around the club. Because LC told him to buck the fuck up and deal with it.

Because he realized that he'd fallen in love with Tanner, which was something Jesse somehow knew would happen.

The only comforting thought was that it appeared that Tanner felt the exact same way.

But when the phone rang at the end of the ninth day, it was the one Damon had been dreading. Having already been on the receiving end of one, it was with a shaking fist that he held the phone to his ear and listened to Rex tell him that *everything was going to be fine*, but there'd been an accident.

"Tanner," he said hoarsely.

"He's in the infirmary."

"What the hell happened?"

"Training exercise that got a little out of hand. He's got a concussion. He hasn't really woken up yet, so they're running some tests." He paused. "Damon, are you still there?"

Damon wanted to be anywhere but on the other end of this

phone call. "Can I come see him?"

"Why do you think I'm calling?"

He'd hung up after Rex told him where to find Tanner and saw LC standing in the doorway, as if some sixth sense had called him there.

LC had taken one look at his face when he'd hung up the phone with Rex and walked out into the club and guided Damon into the truck.

"He'll be fine. We used to get concussions during training all the time," LC reminded him.

"This isn't about us," Damon growled and LC held up his hands in mock surrender.

"I forgot. Everything has to be made into a complete fucking drama."

"Can you drop it?"

"Not until you can. Don't freak him out, okay?"

Damon pushed out of the truck without another word and headed to meet Rex, who led him to the infirmary. Introduced Damon as Tanner's cousin so the doc would let him in.

"He's still out of it. We keep waking him, and the prognosis looks good," the doctor told him. "Staying in for a few days after an injury like this is routine."

And finally—fucking finally—the doctor pushed the curtain back and let Damon in to see Tanner.

He fought the feeling of his knees buckling when he saw Tanner lying unmoving on the bed with all the monitors around him, but he forced himself forward and made a closer inspection.

His right cheekbone was bruised but other than that, Tanner's face remained unblemished. Damon curled his hand into a fist so he wouldn't stroke Tanner's cheek with the doctor still in the room. But when he was left alone a few minutes later with the privacy curtain pulled, Damon reached out and felt for his pulse, strong and sure under his two fingers. Needed to feel it, despite the fact the machines told him Tanner's heartbeat was strong as hell.

He's fine. He's absolutely fine. This was nothing.

And still, his knees felt like they'd buckle any second.

He couldn't do this. Not again. Because it would hurt much more this time.

When had that happened?

"Tanner, damn you," he whispered.

Tanner didn't answer and Damon remained there, holding his hand.

The camouflage paint still lingered on parts of Tanner's face. After a while, Damon took a cloth and wet it, began to gently scrub the marks from his face as if he could wash away all the hurt and confusion...as if he could wipe away the Army from between them and leave everything fresh and new.

Instead, it was messy and confusing for both. Or hell, maybe just for him, because Tanner seemed so damned sure of himself. Of them.

When the hell had he lost total control of the situation?

The thing was, with Tanner, he did lose control, and the worst—the best—part of it was that Damon liked it.

But the fear was too intense, too overwhelming, and he was such a coward he couldn't even stand himself.

He dropped the cloth, stared at Tanner's face like he could memorize it that way.

He knew, no matter what, that he'd never forget all of this, and that made it all the more difficult to leave.

It was like trying to breathe underwater. Everything fucking hurt and Tanner shifted and tried to get comfortable and yeah, that was not working.

The nurses assured him that he was getting a good dose of pain meds. He knew bruised ribs hurt like hell, and his head throbbed in tandem and shit, he wanted to be in his own bed.

He must've been mumbling about that or God knows what because he heard, "Tanner, stop moving—you're going to hurt yourself more."

He hadn't realized he'd been thrashing until he felt the hands on him, stopping him from moving from side to side in search of comfort when there was none.

It was then that he opened his eyes and saw Damon standing over him.

Damon. *Shit.* Who the hell told him about this?

"I have my resources," Damon said, because Tanner had obviously spoken his thoughts out loud. Goddamned drugs.

"Don't want you to see me like this," he mumbled.

Damon stared down at him, brushed some hair from his forehead. "You look fine."

"That's...not what I meant."

Damon didn't say anything.

"I *am* fine, Damon."

"That's what the doctor said."

"He's right." The look on Damon's face, like he'd just seen a ghost, made him ache in places he didn't know his heart held.

"I should go."

Tanner struggled to his elbows, despite the stabbing goddamned pain and Damon asking him if he was crazy. "Then why'd you come here if you're just going to run away?"

"I wanted to make sure you were okay."

"You wanted to make sure I was alive. And now you've decided that this is a great goddamned excuse to not let things work out."

"This isn't the time or the place. But yes, this is over," Damon ground out, the hardest words he'd ever remembered speaking.

"You're right." Tanner sank back heavily onto the pillows, a thin sheet of sweat covering him from that small exertion. "Get the fuck out."

He didn't have to ask twice.

LC was waiting with Rex, but the second he saw Damon, he stood and followed Damon outside.

He couldn't even stop to say thanks to Rex, because he was afraid that if he stopped, he'd turn around and go back. He'd never felt so weak in his entire life.

"It's over," he said finally, once he and LC were back in the club after a tensely silent ride.

LC stared at him steadily, a glint in his eyes that Damon recognized from their days spent in covert ops. "Yeah, I figured you wouldn't have the balls to see it through."

"What the fuck, *Law*?"

At that name, LC blinked hard and balled his fists. "You're scared shitless. And it's not for the reasons you think."

"Christ, you're an asshole," Damon muttered.

"You want to know what your problem is?" LC asked and no, Damon didn't want to but LC would tell him anyway. "You're scared because Tanner takes care of you in a way you've always wanted but you think it means you're weak. You lecture about how strong you need to be to be a sub, but when you realize that you don't mind giving up some of that famous Damon control, you freak."

Damon clenched his jaw. In all the years he'd known LC, the urge to punch the man was never as strong as it was right now. And LC knew that and continued to goad him.

"But right—blame Tanner's job instead. And Jesse. Blame anyone and everyone but who's truly responsible. You."

Damon did grab LC by the front of his shirt this time and LC's eyes blazed. "What the fuck do you want from me, LC?"

"Hurt me if it makes you feel better. Prove I'm right."

Damon let go of his friend and walked out of the club, realizing he hadn't proven anything to anyone at all that day.

Chapter Fourteen

Three days later, Tanner was let out of the hospital. He was still aching badly but it didn't matter. He needed to see Damon.

Damon had been waiting for any excuse and Tanner had just handed it to him on a silver platter. But there was more there that Damon was struggling with. His all-consuming need to protect Tanner and yet, when he couldn't, his gut instinct was to leave him.

He wasn't letting Damon off the damned hook. No, Damon had opened up a whole new world to Tanner, and now it was Tanner's turn to return the favor.

And so he dragged himself into a cab and into the club and pushed through the crowds. Pushed right through the bodyguard who told him he was no longer welcome here.

"You are fucking kidding me, right?"

"No, I'm not." The man stood in front of him, as if that would be enough to stop Tanner. The anger rose up, hot and sharp, and he decked the guy with a swift right hook and walked past him.

"Let him through," LC called above the din and Tanner shook off the hands that attempted to hold him. He strode up to LC, who said, "He's in his office. That was his order, not mine."

"I figured."

"Hey." LC caught him by the elbow before he went down the hall. "Don't go easy on him. That's the last thing he needs."

LC let go when Tanner nodded and continued down the small hallway until he got to the office. He let himself in and slammed the door behind him hard, even as Damon was up out of his seat, cursing a blue streak.

And then he stopped suddenly, and Tanner realized with a start that it was the very first time Damon had ever seen him in uniform. For a few long minutes, Damon simply stared at him and then finally, he found his voice again, his tone angry as hell.

"Shouldn't you still be in the hospital?"

"That's where you want me, isn't it? Because then it'd be easier to handle. Easier to shove me away and treat me like some distant memory." Tanner was advancing and Damon was strangely glued to the spot.

"Why'd you come here?"

"Good to see you too."

Damon didn't look amused and yeah, this was very much like antagonizing a wounded lion, but Tanner was beyond caring.

"I told you it was over," Damon said bluntly.

"I don't take your commands."

"You like some of them well enough."

Tanner nodded at the truth of that statement and Damon continued. "You should go."

"No."

Damon's eyes flashed. "It's not the time to push."

"I think it's the best damned time. Time to start smashing down some goddamned walls of yours. Unless you think you can't handle it." And then Tanner was on him. "I'm not going anywhere, Damon. Because I don't want to. Because you don't really want me to. I don't get it. You were in this world. You understand it. So what's the big goddamned deal? Because from where I'm sitting it's still all about Jesse, even though you're insisting it's not."

Damon turned away, and Tanner took that as a brush-off and grabbed Damon by the shoulder to turn him by force.

Damon reacted, the hard grasp to the shoulder, the touch, made him grab at Tanner and Tanner lashed right back at him, and the fight was on.

The men went down, tumbling bodies entwined as they rolled, hitting the wall first and then the desk as they each got in their punches and sputtered curses...grunting and sweating...and then it changed.

Tanner was hard. So was Damon, and when he managed to get a hand between them to stroke Tanner's cock, Tanner continued to struggle.

"Don't," Tanner grunted. "Can't think when you do that. Can't fucking stay pissed..."

But Damon wasn't pissed any longer—Tanner could see that rolling together this way had gotten Damon worked up to a point where he was beyond the normal control he held over himself. "I don't care what you want right now. It's about my wants."

"About fucking time," Tanner managed to gasp even as Damon moved off him.

"On your knees," Damon commanded and Tanner complied, even though his ribs ached. He wouldn't not follow these orders even if it killed him. Damon yanked his jungle cammy pants down, his boots off, and he was ass-up naked in under a minute.

And suddenly, he was nervous. It was like being a virgin all over again, and it hadn't been that long ago that he'd experienced all of this.

"Please…"

"You think asking nicely's going to save you from this, little boy?" Damon breathed in his ear. "You've been pushing for this since day one. And now you're going to get what you want."

"You're what I want," he whispered, but far too low for Damon to hear.

"Going to make you my little bitch. Is that what you want?"

"Yes."

"Louder."

"Yes, I want to be your little bitch!"

Damon dragged the boy off his knees and over to the couch, pushed him down to sitting. His cock was hard again and he was impatient as all get-out.

He was mesmerized at the jut of Tanner's hipbones, traced them with his thumbs as he licked the head of Tanner's cock and watched the boy jerk.

"Fuck," Tanner growled, and he was so beautiful, lying there, waiting for Damon to take him.

His mouth slid lower, Tanner's legs splayed over Damon's shoulders, his ass spread wide, and Damon tongued his ass and Tanner cursed again and groaned and fucked the air desperately, needing to feel something on his dick.

He'd be reduced to begging soon, Damon knew as his tongue and finger entered Tanner's ass…a knuckle bent to brush the prostate and Tanner was moving, moaning, so Damon went in for the kill, his face buried in Tanner's ass. Tanner's would be buried in his later. Damon would make sure of it.

He heard a soft gasp from Tanner, looked up to see the boy

spread wantonly in a deliciously debauched position. The soft rasp of pressure from Damon's tongue against Tanner's perineum and another gasp—louder this time. His legs spread wide...a hand threaded in Damon's hair.

Unable to hold back, Damon's tongue speared Tanner's hole, leaving the man thrashing against the couch. With his hands firmly holding Tanner's thighs apart, he continued the assault until Tanner was pleading that he needed to come.

Right. Fucking. Now.

There was something delicious about letting the boy attempt to give the commands, letting him run as wild as he wanted to. "Not yet."

"Jesus, Damon, please. Fuck, I..." There was a frantic struggle and then heavy pants. Tanner's muscles strained as Damon kept his thighs opened and his tongue and fingers thrusting in tandem, taking Tanner and claiming him...watching his cock bob, precome leaking.

"Damon, please." Tanner's voice took a slightly higher pitch, even as Damon added a third finger and then a fourth...twisted and licked and realized he was about to come all over himself. So he did at the same time Tanner's orgasm shot through him and for a long moment, both men stared at one another as the sensations of pleasure racked their bodies.

And then Tanner rolled over onto his side, curled in a ball, body shaking from the sensations.

It left his ass open to Damon, who was hard again and entering his already primed hole, filling him because the boy was helpless to stop it. He offered no resistance as Damon slammed into him over and over until he clutched the cushions and got himself onto his knees even as Damon wound a hand in the back of his hair, holding on like Tanner was a wild horse and Damon was digging in the spurs and showing him who was boss.

Tanner was so damned strong—he fought, bucked, and that made it more of a turn-on for Damon as he held him down and listened to him alternately beg and curse.

But ultimately, Tanner could do nothing but try to grab the side of the couch as Damon took him, hard and fast until Tanner was inco-fucking-herent, his ass filled, his body moving with every one of Damon's thrusts.

Damon would leave marks...he wanted to leave marks, especially when he heard the rough, urgent, growl drumming in the back of his throat as he pushed Tanner over an edge he hadn't even known existed.

"You look damned good in uniform," Damon murmured against his ear. Tanner was splayed on the couch under him, his body worn out, and the anger and hurt had dissipated.

He only had another few days of medical leave before he had to be back for mission planning. He'd been so pissed at Damon that he hadn't even thought about the fact that he'd been wearing his cammies, and with the Army still a nearly unreachable subject between them, it had been a damned dangerous move.

Dangerous, but necessary.

"Did I hurt you?" Damon asked when Tanner didn't say anything.

"Yeah, you did."

Damon rolled off him, immediately concerned, and then realized that Tanner wasn't talking physically, despite the toll their earlier fight had taken on his still-sore body. "Fuck, Tanner, I'm..."

Tanner held up his hand to stop Damon from talking. Got

off the couch himself and began to gather his clothes. "Stop saying you're fucking sorry, Damon. I can't deal with it. You want me. You're going to have to find a way to get over this bullshit. Because I don't believe your *sorry* shit anymore."

"Then why come here?" Damon challenged.

"Because I'm not letting you get away with your bullshit excuses anymore. If you don't love me, don't want to be with me, that's fine—I'm a big boy and I can handle it. But I don't know what the hell else is going on between us. This is way beyond Jesse and your fear of me dying. And if I leave for this mission without things resolved between us, I'm not coming back here to you, for my own goddamned sanity. Ball's in your court, the way it's been for the past few weeks. But you needed to see that even though I got hurt, I'm still here. I want to be here. And I wasn't going to let your last memory of me revolve around me passed out in a goddamned hospital bed. Let tonight burn in your memory and we'll see if you're man enough to handle it this time."

And then, just like that first night, he walked out of the club with his clothing in his hand...except this time, he let the tears fall before he got to the car.

Chapter Fifteen

LC hadn't meant to watch Damon fucking Tanner in his office. But he'd waited outside the office, not wanting the men to kill each other. When he'd caught sight of what was really happening, he couldn't stop. Because seeing Tanner spread on the couch, Damon kneeling between his legs...it was him and Styx all over again. Styx humping the shit out of him in the back room of Greg's old club, Styx holding him down, taking him so fucking hard he'd felt it for weeks in the way only good sex could make you ache.

The next morning, Styx had been gone.

Tanner would be gone next week—and hopefully not forever—but there were only so many promises a man could keep.

LC alternately wanted to warn Tanner to stay away from Damon and pray that he stayed. And when he could tear his eyes from the beautiful men, he'd walked back into the club and as far away from the office as possible, even though he could still hear the sex for a long while.

That had been four hours ago, and he knew Tanner had walked out of the club buck naked, according to Renn, about three hours earlier. And no way was LC going to find Damon. Let the asshole come to him.

Which he did, but not until two days later, forty-eight

hours in which LC didn't see his friend once. And still, the first thing out of Damon's mouth was, "I didn't think you liked to watch."

"Fuck you."

Damon backed off then, because he saw the fierceness in LC's eyes, knew he'd been ruminating on Styx and thought for the millionth time about hunting him down and killing him for what he'd done to LC.

Because he couldn't have LC not speaking to him, not now, when Tanner wasn't either.

Damn you, Jesse. Why couldn't you leave well enough alone?

"How are things with Paulo?" he asked, because he couldn't help himself.

"There's no thing with Paulo."

"I heard he caught you outside the club playing secret spy killer."

"Are you pissed you didn't? Because we're not all under your control, sir," LC said through gritted teeth and Damon could still see him in the jungle, face painted, the same precision in his bearing. "Why don't you focus on your own relationship?"

"Because you and I both know it's not going to work."

"Tell him, Damon. Tell him everything and give him a chance to see if he's strong enough to handle your shit."

"Jesse wasn't."

"Not that you ever gave him the opportunity, but no, I think it would've killed Jesse to know you've been in pain for so long. But Tanner's not Jesse. I think he can handle what you dish out. He's proven that so far." LC stared at him. "In this relationship, you're actually the weak one and you're terrified he's going to find that out."

"The attacks have thrown me. You know that."

"JP can't get to you—not in the same way he did."

"I should've left it where he couldn't ever get to anyone like that."

"We couldn't find him. You were spending every spare minute on vengeance and that almost took you down. You had to let it go. Greg always told us not to dwell on our mistakes, just not to repeat them," LC reminded him. "Let me take care of it."

"It's too dangerous for either of us. Especially now that Paulo's involved. And don't blame me for that—he was circling your ass before I got involved."

LC just shook his head. "Call Tanner."

"What if it's too late?"

"It's only too late when someone's in the ground. And even then, you can always find redemption."

So Damon did the only thing he could. He left a message for Tanner to meet him at the club that night. It was Monday, which meant it was closed, which would work perfectly for what Damon had in mind. And now, it was a matter of waiting, impatiently, to see if Tanner would give him yet another chance.

He wouldn't screw up this time.

When he heard Tanner's bike pull up just before midnight, Damon practically tripped over himself getting outside to make sure he got in safely.

Tanner just shook his head, like he knew what Damon was doing but he didn't say a word. Not until they got inside, anyway.

"What's up?" Tanner looked around the empty club and back at Damon. "I thought you couldn't deal with this—with us—with my Army shit. So what's changed?"

"I'm trying, Tanner. Fuck it all, I'm trying."

Tanner didn't look convinced.

"Tonight—this—it's not about me. I'm going to help you keep your original promise. Make a good memory to erase a questionable one."

"I have a lot of good memories with you."

"There's room for more. Trust me."

"I've been trying, Damon."

He heard the slight break in the boy's voice and he knew he had one last chance to make this right, to prove to Tanner he was in it for the long haul. "Please. I have no right to ask, but I'm going to."

Tanner nodded after a pause long enough to give Damon heart palpitations. With that, he led Tanner through the empty club and to Room Four.

Tanner paused at the edge of the room, understanding the significance. Watched Damon walk in and press the button to expose the room to the entire club, and even though no one was there to watch them...Tanner could still feel eyes on him.

And when Damon turned to look at him with a heavy lust in his eyes, Tanner's cheeks flushed. "Come on in."

Tanner still hesitated, but Damon went to meet him halfway and finally, Tanner stepped inside the room.

"Are you ready?"

"I'm ready, Damon."

"Yes, you are, sweet boy." He wrapped a hand around the back of his neck, pulling him close for a kiss. He let his tongue explore Tanner's mouth, their kiss getting more intense as the moments went on. And as he kissed, he tugged off Tanner's pants, broke from him for a second to pull Tanner's shirt off too and pulled Tanner's naked body back to his fully clothed one.

Tanner was rubbing against him and Damon knew he loved that, loved being naked while Damon had everything on and so he tugged him to the padded mattress on the floor, and they ended up rolling around for a few minutes before Tanner pulled back, breathing hard. He glanced over at the bench but he turned back to Damon quickly.

"That first night, I should've protected you."

"It's okay, Damon." He got up to move toward the bench but Damon pulled him back.

"No scenes. No bindings. You don't need them." Damon stripped his clothes off while Tanner watched. "Neither do I."

But then he reached in his pocket and pulled out the collar with the skull and crossbones, the one Jesse had made Tanner request. But Damon didn't put it on Tanner. Instead, he placed it on the bench Tanner had lain on that first night and then turned his attention back to the boy.

He laid his weight on Tanner, their naked bodies rubbing together as they kissed. Tanner was strong enough to half roll him and for a moment, Damon reveled in the feeling of strength, the way Tanner held him. Kissed him.

Damon fisted their cocks together, rubbed them as one entity. Neither of them would last long if he didn't take the edge off for both of them. And Damon wanted all night.

Tanner hadn't been sure about coming to Crave at all, but in the end, he knew he had to give Damon another chance.

He was so fucking glad he did. No one made him feel like this...no one ever would, and goddamn, he wanted this for fucking ever.

Damon moved down his body as Tanner watched, spread his legs and took his cock in his mouth.

"Not gonna last," he rasped out, but it didn't matter— Damon wanted him to come immediately. And Tanner's cock seemed to do whatever the hell the man wanted.

Damon's eyes were dark as he stared up at him, his beard scraping along Tanner's inner thighs and Tanner groaned. Damon licked his balls, mouthing one then the other, and Tanner could almost hear the applause from the crowd, but this time, they'd be privy to Damon pleasuring him, his legs spread wide.

He came in a hot rush down Damon's throat with no warning, his hips pressed to the ground by Damon's hands, a white-hot light behind his eyes from the orgasm. But Damon wasn't stopping. He acted like Tanner could come again instantly and Christ, he was still hard enough to even though that seemed impossible.

But with Damon, it seemed as if anything was possible.

And then Damon climbed up to him again, spread his thighs wide as he kneeled in front of him. Tanner had been prepared to turn onto his hands and knees.

"What are you going to do to me?" he asked.

"Spread you. Watch you open for me, willingly."

And he was spread wantonly, hole exposed, heavy sac hanging, cock jutting to his belly.

"What are you going to do to me, Damon?" he asked again.

"I'm going to take you again. Make you come."

And it was then that Tanner understood what Damon planned. He would take him from the front in a way that would've been far too intimate for either of them mere days ago.

"Like this? You're sure?" Tanner asked.

"Yeah, just like this. I've wanted to. I just...couldn't. It wasn't right until now," Damon told him.

Tonight, it was perfect.

Tanner swallowed hard. Looked up at Damon and gave him a half smile. "I wanted this too. I just thought...maybe..."

"It's time." And, as Damon settled in, Tanner splayed his thighs open farther to accommodate Damon's body, watched his cock, slicked and ready, begin the long, slow, painfully goddamned delicious slide into his ass.

"You okay, baby boy?"

"I'm already here...you can drop the seduction shit."

"Never."

Damon grinned at the way Tanner snapped through his vulnerability, and Tanner wondered if Damon would always be able to see through him so clearly.

It seemed only fair, since Tanner could now read Damon like a book, saw the slight tremor in Damon's body as he prepared to rock them into a screaming, sweaty, oh-so-tangled mess and Tanner was so ready.

"I've been aching for you," he said, and Damon hissed, pushed in farther. Tanner breathed through the pinch of pain, knowing what came behind it was the best. "So big...filling me...yeah, Damon...put it all the way in."

Damon threw his head back and he did, until his cock brushed Tanner's prostate and made him see stars. Damon came down on his palms and Tanner's legs locked around his waist as if they had a mind of their own, pushing, urging Damon to just move.

"Impatient. Always pushing," Damon grunted.

"Yeah—fuck me, Damon. Take me here...in front of

everyone."

Damon's eyes turned liquid with a lust that was unmistakable. "You'd let me, wouldn't you? You'd spread your legs anywhere I asked you to."

"Yes."

"On the bar, in the middle of a crowded Saturday night, people all around you, watching, listing to every sound you make."

"Yes...yes," he gasped, close to incoherence at Damon's little trip down fantasy lane, and he could imagine the men around him now as Damon took him, claiming him like a prize.

"Yes, baby, you're my prize," Damon said and Christ, Tanner was babbling everything that came into his head out loud as Damon's cock slammed his sweet spot with precision, Damon's body giving his no quarter, no room to rest...his eyes never leaving Tanner's face. "You'll always be my prize."

Tanner nodded, his hands clutching the bed. "Fuck me, Damon. Harder. Now."

Spurred on by Tanner's command, Damon did, lifted one of Tanner's thighs so he could drive in more deeply, saw by Tanner's expression that he'd hit his mark.

Tanner tried to gain quarter where he could but his arms couldn't find one spot—they moved from Damon's back to his hips and then the sheets. Damon was like a charging bull, an unstoppable force, and Tanner couldn't do anything but receive the fucking that was fast and hard and so damned hot.

"Damon...stay with me."

Damon knew what he was asking—and he was ready to promise it now.

"Yes, Tanner...will stay."

Tanner came when Damon said that, hard enough to cry

out with surprise, and Damon followed, his body shuddering over Tanner's. Tanner clutched him, arms and legs wrapped around the bigger man, face buried against his neck, both their bodies slick from sweat.

"You kept your promise. You're free, sweet boy."

Tanner was...but he didn't want to be free from Damon. He pulled back to look at Damon. "Don't let me go...please."

To his horror, the tears rose again.

Damon didn't tell him to shush or stop, simply held him tight and let the emotions flood out until he was spent. Emotionally. Sexually.

For the first time, he knew he was right where he needed to be. Released. Held. Renewed.

"Let it go, sweet boy...let it all go."

And finally, Tanner did.

Tanner lay in Damon's arms for a long time after his breakthrough. Neither had been able to move when the sex was finished and now, neither had the desire to untangle themselves.

Tanner shifted first, but only to latch his mouth to Damon's nipple, sucking it to a hard pebble while Damon twined his fingers in Tanner's hair.

"You want more, sweet boy?" he whispered and Tanner looked up at him, nipple still in his mouth. Nodded and just like that, Damon knew he was totally, one hundred percent completely gone. In love, and all bets were off.

Damon reached down to play with Tanner's cock, deciding what to do with his boy now, how to make Tanner get his rocks off.

So many ways...and it felt like they had so little time. "So much I want to do with you, Tanner. So much, if you'll let me."

Tanner's eyes were wet with desire...and with trust. Watching Tanner come apart was so satisfying, pride flooded Damon that he could bring the boy to this state with his cock...his touch...his kiss.

He was enough. And finally, he felt like he'd lived up to the promise Tanner had made Jesse.

Chapter Sixteen

Damon and Tanner holed up in Damon's loft for two days straight, coming up for air only to order take-out, which LC delivered to them, leaving it outside the door after knocking.

Good, that was damned good. Now there was one last thing LC had to solve. The attacker was someone LC had decided to take on single-handedly, and he'd been outside both nights, using himself as bait, and nothing.

Still he'd felt eyes on him last night for the first time, and he'd learned from a young age to never doubt his instincts. And tonight, he'd try again—there was no way this would go away that easily. Not when he'd stepped out back this morning and found the charm in the alley. A gold horn.

His stomach tightened because he knew that symbol. JP always wore a horn on his necklace...and he'd left it on Damon's body out in the alley that night so long ago when LC hadn't been there to protect his friend.

No, LC had been with Styx and Damon had gone out on his own. LC knew Damon was going to do so, but when he was with Styx, he tended to forget his own goddamned name. Which was why he couldn't bear to think of himself as Law any longer after the attack on Damon.

Damon had lost so much that night—they both had. LC hadn't seen Styx again for months and after that, it had only been sporadically. And now, their past was coming back to haunt them in the cruelest way possible.

JP was only a couple of years older than LC and Damon—big and strong and mean—and apparently, he hadn't changed. And it appeared he was now taunting them—or LC himself—and at this point, it didn't matter. He'd known all along who it was but hadn't wanted to admit it out loud.

He couldn't believe the grudge could've gone on this long.

Right before he went outside, he closed his eyes and pressed his palms and forehead to the door, letting the cold seep through, shoving his emotions down. They would not help him. And then he slipped outside in his hooded sweatshirt, prepared to act drunk, calling out behind him to the empty hallway, "Diner run—be back later," and he let the door close with a soft click behind him.

And then he began to walk down the alleyway, stumbling a little bit. JP was out here tonight—he'd bet his life on it. Delta had honed his instincts and while time softened them a bit, during a time like this, he was a soldier once again.

But he couldn't let on that he knew and so he left himself vulnerable. Refused to turn around and call out JP's name.

And he'd gotten halfway down the alley when it happened. The slam to the back of the head—he'd heard the whoosh in the air and was able to move fast so he didn't take the full brunt of the blow.

Still, it was enough to bring him down. Temporarily stunned, he struggled to sit up, to move away from the footsteps he heard coming toward him. Continued playing drunk, because he wanted the upper hand in this, wanted to make certain that this guy would never do anything like this again.

He didn't see anyone yet, looked over and saw the heavy

boomerang that had hit him in the head.

No wonder he hadn't seen it coming. Fuck.

It was then that he heard the familiar voice. Even though it wasn't unexpected, a chill went up LC's spine anyway. "You look good, Law."

"You don't call me that," he said through clenched teeth and JP laughed. JP—the man who'd been the ringleader years ago when Damon was attacked. JP, who'd aged hard but still looked big and mean as hell, and was leaning over him now with a knife to his throat.

He still remembered being cornered by JP and his gang of assholes when he was seventeen, in an alley eerily similar to this one. JP, who had always hit on him, had gotten angry when LC told him that JP wasn't his type.

He'd fought not to get taken, knew he would have if Styx hadn't come to his rescue. Styx had beaten the shit out of the assholes, but JP had run away. And since they couldn't bring the police sniffing around in their direction, they'd let it go. Traveled together when they went out clubbing. Never left with strange men.

JP was watching him remember. He was smiling—the bastard was smiling. "Baby, you're going to call me daddy before we're through here. Because that's what I wanted all along. Wrong man was in the wrong place."

LC's blood ran cold. "This isn't about Damon?"

"It never was. It was always about you, Law. Always."

It was always about you, Law. The words echoed in his mind as he lunged up and went for JP, the pain in his head nothing compared to the one he'd felt all these years. In that moment, JP was everyone who'd ever hurt him.

But the past welled up too hard—the memories getting in

the way of the fight, and JP proved to be very well trained—knew a lot of the same fighting techniques LC did. LC would guess military. JP was broader than he was—muscle-bound—and that plus his training would make him a fierce opponent and explain why the men JP attacked hadn't had a chance of getting away.

Still, the icy rain that started moments earlier made it difficult for either man to get their footing. JP managed to slam a fist into LC's left cheekbone. The feeling of bones breaking—of pain—was oddly familiar. Brought LC back to another time and place he didn't want to be.

But he was no longer a child and there was a reason he was being hit here. It wasn't blind, drunken rage—in JP's mind, he'd been slighted, and in the hands of this psychopathic asshole, LC knew he had to fight back this time, and he would.

LC tackled him to the frozen blacktop—he heard the crunch of their bodies as they went down. But he was still disoriented from the blow to the head, more so than he'd originally thought, and he struggled to keep the upper hand. The pent-up anger he felt could do brutal things—LC had been on both sides of it, and he hadn't wanted to be in this place again, ever.

If he was going to get the answers he sought from JP, he'd have to not kill him first.

Rolling over and playing dead was so not in his nature, but he'd been pretending for so long already. And so he let JP use an arm to stronghold him to the ground, where LC lay prone.

JP rolled him immediately, hovered over him and yeah, the brush cut screamed military. LC also saw the outline of the dog tags under his shirt.

"Damon wanted it," JP told him with a hand across LC's throat, and things were getting fuzzy.

LC saw Damon's face as it had been all those years ago swim in front of his eyes.

"They told me they'd tell the police I wanted it. And fuck, Law, I was begging for it at points," Damon said, his voice urgent.

"Because of the drug. That wasn't you asking for it—you didn't consent."

"I know Damon went looking for me and the other men from that night," JP told him now. "Damon doesn't scare me. I didn't run from him—I enlisted. When I went back to the old neighborhood, I heard Damon had been looking for me. That you'd come with him."

LC managed to get his hands under JP's arm, enough to pull some air into his lungs. "Then why hurt those other men—why not come directly for me?"

"Because it was fun watching you try to put two and two together. You and that detective practically screwing against the wall." He laughed harshly. "That's not the way to do a watch, boy. Were you not taking me seriously?"

"I take you very seriously."

The gun clicked then, pressed to the side of LC's head. "Get up and start walking."

"I'm not going anywhere with you, so you might as well kill me here."

"Baby, I was just trying to give you a little comfort. But if you'd like it out here in the raw, that's fine. Either way, our first time will be special."

"Like you did to Damon. And the other men out here."

"They all took it like babies. You'll take it like a man when I fuck you."

It was all LC needed to hear. In seconds, he was up, letting the rage explode out of him, and JP looked shocked as his arm was pushed to the ground and the gun clattered on the blacktop. And then it was LC's turn to hold his arm across JP's throat, choking the life out of him.

"I'll kill you for what you did to Damon—to the others. How many boys' lives did you ruin?" he asked JP, watched the man's eyes bulge and his face redden. "I will fucking kill you right here."

"LC, stop." Tanner, pulling at him, attempting to yank him away from JP, who was still struggling.

LC didn't break his position. "You don't understand."

"It's not worth going to jail for killing him."

"Self-defense." He refused to let himself be taken off JP until he saw him slip into unconsciousness. It was only then that JP's face morphed into LC's father's face, and LC finally let go.

He would not be like that man. Ever. But he'd come damned close tonight.

JP's not an innocent.

But LC always knew—had lived with the fact that he had the blood of a killer inside of him.

If it hadn't been for Tanner, he might've proven that true tonight.

"What was this about... Did he attack you?" Tanner asked as LC shifted unsteadily on his feet. Tanner held him up by the shoulders.

"Not me, Tanner." LC stared at him. "Do you understand? What JP did years ago wasn't to me...I was the one who discovered Damon, in the alley. And JP...he was one of them."

"One of them?" Tanner echoed. "This guy attacked Damon?"

"Years ago—when he was a kid. Younger than you. Makes sense now, doesn't it?" LC asked. "He'd never tell you willingly—never told Jesse—would never tell anyone at all. And he needs to if he's got a shot at any kind of real relationship."

"Jesus, LC..."

"Don't you dare tell him you know."

"How am I supposed to bring it up, then?"

"You're a smart boy—you'll figure it out," he said, right before the dizziness began to overtake him. He remembered Tanner calling his name, catching him...and then nothing.

He wasn't sure how long he was out, but when he opened his eyes, Damon was standing over him and he was inside the club.

He heard the ambulance sirens in the distance. Damon's face was white as shit.

"I'm not going to the hospital."

"The fuck you're not. What the hell were you thinking?" Damon demanded, even as Paulo was asking the same thing from the other side of him.

"I don't need all this fuss. I'm fine, dammit." But as LC went to haul himself up, his head spun and yeah, that JP asshole had hit him harder than he'd thought. Damon caught him and helped him lie back down. And Paulo walked away, pushing out the alley door.

Damon remained, staring down at him. "You have a concussion. You're going in for observation. I can't lose another person, Law."

Law. Jesus. "I'll go, Damon. I'll go. And it's over now. I got it all on tape."

Damon's jaw was clenched tightly. "Yeah, it's over."

"He's going to jail. Finally." He paused. "Tanner stopped me

211

from killing him. He did the right thing."

When Damon first came outside, he looked like he'd seen a ghost. He must've been as pale as LC and couldn't stop staring between his friend and the man LC had beaten to a pulp on the ground.

Tanner was holding LC, and Damon took LC from him, said he'd wait inside with the man.

"Tanner, stay with him and wait for the police," he'd said hoarsely, gestured to JP and Tanner agreed. He called Paulo in case the detective hadn't heard and left him a message.

And then Tanner checked the pulse on the man on the ground. JP would probably need the hospital first, judging by the ring of bruises around his throat but then jail for sure. LC had filmed the incident, thanks to hidden cameras in the alley.

And when Damon went in the ambulance with LC, Tanner had waited for Paulo and gave a statement as to what he'd seen—LC defending himself—while Paulo's gaze flicked over his face, searching for the truth.

"He knew this man," Paulo said.

"You'll have to ask him."

"I'm asking you what he said."

"He didn't say anything. He was busy fighting for his life." Tanner stuffed his hands in his pockets, LC's words still echoing in his mind.

Not me, Tanner... Do you understand? What JP did years ago wasn't to me. I was the one who discovered Damon, in the alley. And JP...he was one of them.

God...Damon...all of this was happening at once. No wonder the man had been so fearful about Tanner getting hurt...being taken advantage of by Joe and Hunt. It was all adding up now.

He told Paulo, "Go see LC. Talk to him." Because eventually, Paulo would see the film, and Tanner suspected LC would rather tell him first.

Paulo nodded. "I plan on it. First, I'm going to escort this asshole to the hospital and get his confession."

Styx watched from the shadows as Law slept, monitors beeping in tandem with the thudding in his own chest. He fought the urge to go to him, to hold his hand, to comfort him.

Maybe they were too far gone. Irreparable. That's what Law had told him all those years ago.

Dammit, he should've come when he'd called, should've known that something was really wrong.

And Law was taking matters into his own hands, something he'd done for as long as they'd known each other.

Move forward. Go to him.

From the curtain on the empty side of the room, he remained hidden, feet glued to the floor instead.

And then the door opened and a man came in. Young, handsome, and he headed straight for the bed. Took Law's hand and held it and damn it all if Law didn't open his eyes and look right at him.

Too late. These days, Styx always found himself a day late and a dollar short and he had no one but himself to blame.

And still, he couldn't help but notice that Law looked to the curtain and stared at it for a long moment before turning his attention back to the blond man who still held onto his hand.

"What the hell happened?" Paulo asked, his voice steady over the beeping of the machines that surrounded him.

LC didn't remember much about the ambulance ride or being admitted. Knew that he'd been a pain in the ass when the doctor was trying to assess his condition but hell, at least LC knew he was okay.

Would've been hard to be such an asshole if he'd been dying.

LC shifted in the bed, stared into Paulo's concerned dark blue eyes. "Are you asking as a detective?"

"As your friend."

LC tried to overt his gaze but Paulo wouldn't let him, used a single finger under his chin and barely any pressure to force LC's eyes to his. "Did he hurt you?"

"I'm in the fucking hospital."

"Not what I meant, you asshole. You fucking stupid asshole." Paulo's words were harsh but his tone—the look on his face—wasn't. Not at all, and it made LC feel worse about being such a dick.

He swallowed, hard. "JP tried once. And he hurt Damon."

"I know—I saw the tape."

"I couldn't stop him back then because I..." He paused, then let the words rush out, blaming it on the pain meds they'd given him. "I couldn't help him then because I was too busy screwing around with someone I thought I'd be with forever."

The fact that Styx hadn't stuck around made that so much worse.

"You're talking about the guy you can't get over."

"The past has a way of not staying put when it's supposed to." LC winced as he tried to sit up, brushed off Paulo's offer to

214

help.

Paulo took his hand back though. "You're a mess."

"Tell me something I don't know," he muttered, grabbed the ginger ale with the ice chips with his free hand. "Gotta get out of here."

"They're keeping you overnight."

"Shit." He lay back on the pillows. Damon and Tanner had an awful lot of talking to do. No doubt they needed their privacy...and even though LC wanted out, wanted to beg Paulo to take him to his apartment, he couldn't do that to either of them.

"Are you ever going to tell me about the guy or am I wasting my time competing with a ghost?" Paulo asked.

"It's complicated."

"Sounds pretty simple to me. You won't let go of the past because you're scared to move forward and find out you might actually be happy."

"I'm not scared," LC said through gritted teeth. "And what the hell—why do you care so much?"

"I don't know. I guess some things just happen." Paulo looked as surprised as LC felt. "I didn't expect you to turn into more than a fantasy. But when I'm with you...it's better than that. And that never happens."

"Don't do this, please. I don't...I can't let it go any further."

Paulo nodded, let go of his hand. "Got it, loud and clear."

"I still want to...hang out. Be friends."

"I'll believe it when I see it." Paulo's words weren't unkind but LC felt them harder than a punch to the jaw.

"How are you so sure...about me?" LC asked. He didn't know why he couldn't just let Paulo leave.

"I don't know. It's ridiculous. I push, you run. I come after you."

"Thrill of the chase."

"Ah, LC, I guess I'm old enough to know better."

"You don't know how I grew up—what I'm like."

"I know more than you realize." He touched the bruise under LC's eye gently. "You take care of yourself."

LC's throat was too tight to say anything else, and he could only watch Paulo leave.

Tanner let the police do their job while he went inside the club and waited, wishing he could've gone with Damon and LC.

What the hell was he going to do—force Damon to tell him everything?

Yeah, because that's your only chance at healing him, the way he healed you.

And so he paced and waited and finally Damon pushed through the doors of the club, looking just as pale as he had earlier.

"How's LC?"

"He's fine. They'll keep him, but he's going to be fine." Damon acted like if he repeated that enough, it would be true. "Paulo's with him."

"As his lover or a cop?"

Damon grimaced. "Little of both." Then he turned and locked the front and back doors tight, set the alarms. "I need some sleep."

"Come on." Tanner tugged him gently up the stairs to the loft, but he had no intention of letting Damon sleep. And when they got upstairs, Damon slumped onto the bed, and Tanner went over and knelt down in front of him. Unlaced his boots and took them off, massaged Damon's feet and calves while the man watched him.

"Good to me," he mumbled. "Too good to me."

Instead of commenting on that, Tanner asked, "How did LC know that guy?"

"The same way I did."

Tanner stood and retrieved a bottle of Jack Daniels and Damon took a grateful slug. And then Tanner sat next to Damon on the bed and said, "Tell me."

"I don't want to," he said quietly. "Please, Tanner...I don't want to tell you."

"I know. But I didn't want to talk about Jesse either, and you made me. You made me do a lot of things for my own good and you were right about all of them. And I know I'm right about this."

Damon took another long sip of the JD, letting it burn all the way down. It would take away the pain, the numbness...maybe it would make him strong enough to get the whole thing out once and for all. "There's so much you don't know. That you shouldn't know about me."

"I know that you loved Jesse...and that you know me better than I know myself."

Damon stared at Tanner. "You're brave. Brave and strong and you deserve so much better than me."

"No way, Damon. I deserve you. Want you," Tanner whispered. "I know you want me too."

He was right—so right. And this was truly his final barrier. His past, come back to do more than haunt him. His past had literally walked into his life and LC had nearly killed the man for him. "I couldn't even look at JP. I'm stronger than he is now...and I still couldn't look at him."

"What did he do to you?"

Damon closed his eyes and felt Tanner take one of his hands into his. Squeezed it and then Damon started with his story.

"I was eighteen. Stupid. Thought I'd been around the block enough to know everything." He paused, could picture himself walking into the club, breaking his and LC's pact to do everything together when it came to clubbing, since that wasn't Styx's scene at all.

But LC had been with Styx that night, and Damon hadn't wanted to break up their night together. He'd been sure LC and Styx would be together forever—the way those men looked at one another, it always made him jealous and hopeful that he could find that for himself. "Styx left that night and LC didn't see him again for a while. It started the pattern of Styx appearing and disappearing, and LC finally had enough. Now, it's been over ten years and Styx hasn't tried to get in touch. It was just another memory that got ruined that night."

"That's the reason LC pushes Paulo away," Tanner said and Damon nodded.

"He never got over Styx. Never will, it seems like. He also feels guilty as shit for not being with me that night, although he never admits that to me because he knows it'll make me angry. He has no reason to feel guilt—I did it to myself. I was stupid." He paused. "I was too restless to stay home. And I went to a club—leather and chains. Thought I could take care of myself. God, was I fucking wrong. From the second I walked in, I was bait."

He could still remember the catcalls, the feeling that he'd

walked into the wrong place at the right time for the predators that followed him. "I got propositioned right away. I took a shot because I was nervous—thought I was safe because I took it right from the bartender. I didn't know he was in on it."

"You were drugged."

He looked at Tanner. "Yeah."

"Jesus, Damon...when you found me..."

"Yeah." He couldn't say anything else, couldn't think about what he'd saved Tanner from. It had just been important that he'd saved him.

"They hurt you when you couldn't fight."

"They took me into the back room. At first, there were only two of them—they were all right. They got me hot. And then they tied me down," he said, saw Tanner's jaw twitch. "Chains. There was no way to get out—and I didn't have any of the training I have now. I fought like the street kid I was. But I couldn't do anything."

It was something Damon tried to block out completely and was rarely successful.

"A gang rape," Tanner whispered.

"Yes. There were at least five of them, including JP, who walked in after I was tied down. Told me he couldn't wait to make me his. I knew he'd tried to do the same thing to LC a few years earlier but I never thought... Christ, the guy's psychotic. He was the ringleader of all of it. I wasn't the first one he did it to and I wasn't the last, either. And all I could think of when it was happening was, *I'm glad it's not LC*."

"It must've been so horrible."

Damon shrugged as though it wasn't, but Tanner would know better. "I was in and out of consciousness. There was nothing I could do. LC found me a couple of hours later—they'd dumped me in the alley naked with my clothes dumped on top of me. He got me to the ER. He stayed with me until I healed— physically, at least. That's why he didn't tell me about the attacks right away—but neither of us thought it could be JP. I shouldn't have let him get away."

"You went after the rest of them?"

"Damn straight. Took me years, but I got my own brand of justice on most of them." Damon didn't want to tell Tanner what that had entailed. "The weasel JP ran and hid and then LC and I knew we needed to let it rest."

"You couldn't have known he'd do this."

"I should have. People don't change."

But Tanner did so to the subject. "So, in this club, in your life, you make sure to retain all the control so no one else can ever get hurt again," Tanner said.

"It sounds so simple when you say it. And I'm so fucking stupid to think I can control anything," Damon muttered.

"It's not stupid at all." Tanner's voice was as raw as Damon felt. Tanner's hand stroked across his cheek, his shoulders. "I'm so sorry, Damon. Sorry that happened to you. But trying to control everything doesn't make the bad stuff not happen. And I don't want to lose you because you're always afraid that bad stuff will happen to me."

Damon nodded, wondered if Tanner was going to just walk out now. It had been what he thought he wanted, but he'd been so wrong.

"I think you'd be a Dom anyway," Tanner continued. "You were submissive for me when I asked you to put on the cuffs, but you never really submitted."

No, submission had never been in him. "The attack had nothing to do with sex. Everything to do with power. JP was the golden boy of the club scene for a little while. And then he got a little older and he started to get pushed to the side. Couldn't get everything or everyone he wanted like he'd been used to and decided that being feared would be better than being ignored. In those days, it was much harder to be believed in a situation like that."

"It's over. He can't hurt you or anyone else," Tanner said fiercely.

"I didn't want to tell you. I don't want you to look at me with pity."

"I could never look at you that way."

"If you're doing this because you think Jesse wanted it...Jesse didn't always know what people needed. He wasn't always right. Just because something worked for him...I want you to know that you need someone strong, you don't necessarily need a Dom," Damon said quietly.

"What do you need?" Tanner asked, his hand resting on Damon's lower back. "Do you need a good fucking, Damon? Because I'm your guy."

Damon sucked in a breath at the dirty boy's words. Goddamn him...this was not the same man who walked into his club straight from combat and allowed himself to be strapped down.

This was a boy who liked to be ridden hard...and Damon would normally put him away wet for certain.

But now, Tanner pushed Damon down after taking the bottle from his hand and putting it on the ground. He leaned over him, stroked his cheek.

"Let me fix this for you. Let me make it better," Tanner whispered and Damon knew the boy had embedded himself so deeply in his heart that there was no getting him out now without forcibly ripping him from his chest.

221

"You can't."

"Let me try. Because you haven't been able to do it for yourself."

Tanner's hands were forceful...insistent as he pulled Damon's shirt off, and then his jeans, leaving him in boxer briefs and feeling more naked than if he actually was. But he wasn't protesting the way he normally would have.

Could he really let this happen? "Tanner, look—"

"You're afraid to let go with me."

"That's not true."

"Yeah, it is. Because you'd have to let me slay you—and you're afraid of what that might mean."

Little bastard was right...and he continued, murmuring, "You want to violate me in every possible way...and I want the same from you. I want to fuck you and suck you...hear my name on your lips."

"I never told anyone this. Not even Jesse," Damon whispered. "If he knew—if he felt it, he never said. And I don't like to burden anyone with my shit."

"Sharing burdens makes them better." Tanner kissed Damon's neck. "Please, let me help you."

He knew what Tanner wanted, what he thought would help. And maybe it would. "I'm—"

"Scared. Yeah, I know. But you trust me, right?"

"With my life, Tanner. So go ahead...fuck me. Make it right."

Tanner gave him a small smile. "And if you want me to stop..."

"I'll tell you. Just like that."

Damon closed his eyes and prepared to let Tanner have his

body.

Damon was trembling. Even as Tanner laid a hand on his stomach, it got worse. "Tie me down."

"No."

"It's going to be the only way."

"Bullshit." Tanner's voice was raw...husky. "You'll let me. You'll put your arms around me...and you'll look me in the eye and know it's me inside of you."

"I might hurt you." He was worried he would flash back, slam Tanner off him.

"But you won't." And then Tanner kissed him, slow and deep, letting his hand wander to Damon's cock, stroking and kissing and calming him with the touch until Damon started to relax into the familiar feelings of pleasure.

He would have to lose himself in that in order for this to work at all. Watched as the boy—his boy—sucked his nipples, stroked his belly and his balls, licked his cock and finally spread Damon's thighs as Tanner took him with one finger and then two.

"You're treating me like a fucking virgin."

Tanner smiled, a lazy, heated grin, and he didn't stop spreading Damon with his fingers, circling, scissoring, until Damon was moving to his rhythm, unable to complain about anything. With four fingers inside of him, Damon felt the pleasant burn. Dug his fingers into Tanner's biceps and closed his eyes.

"Open your eyes, Damon—look at me."

There was no mistaking the order and Damon followed it.

"You're not going anyplace else inside your head. You're staying here with me," Tanner admonished as he mounted

Damon, held his thighs apart and slowly, so slowly, began to enter him. "You're watching me fuck you...letting me take you...wanting me to."

Damon could only nod as the pressure built. God, he was like a fucking virgin again, so tight and scared and Tanner leaned forward and kissed him, over and over, until Damon relaxed enough to let Tanner bury himself deep.

"Yeah, that's it. I'm going to move, Damon...and you're coming along for the ride."

He opened his mouth to protest, to tell Tanner that this was a mistake, but when Tanner began to rock his hips in earnest, Damon knew he didn't want to turn back.

Tanner plunged his cock in and out of Damon, pulling out almost completely and then sliding all the way back in, did that enough times so Damon was stretched and ready. And then, when Tanner began to really take him, there was no censoring his speech—it flooded from his mouth as the tension drained from his body and everything was about his dick...his ass...Tanner, deep inside, driving in a relentless pace.

"You're going to make me crave you."

"Good," Tanner panted. "Makes...two of us."

Their thighs slapped and Damon was well aware of the tears that rolled down his cheeks as Tanner took him—well and hard and in a way that washed all the bad memories from him. Their hands were wound together, Tanner holding Damon down but both of them holding each other. Exactly the way it was meant to be.

"More, Tanner," Damon said, and Tanner complied, because there wasn't anything he wouldn't do for the brave man below him.

As he took Damon, aggressiveness and submissiveness fought for control inside of him...it seemed to come out in a perfect blend, because Damon moaned under his touch. It was a heady feeling, making the bigger man tremble like that... It was something Tanner didn't treat lightly.

He had a responsibility to Damon, to his body and his heart. He acknowledged that, accepted it. And then he made Damon his, the same way Damon had claimed him, over and over, for the past weeks.

"Mine," he told the man underneath him. Bit him on the shoulder and flexed his hips to drive himself deeper inside of him. "Say it."

"Yours, sweet boy...all goddamned yours." Damon's voice was rough, and he was holding Tanner tightly, arms and legs wrapped around him as they both roared toward orgasm, calling each other's names into the night.

Chapter Seventeen

Tanner left two days later. At first, there were lots of emails and text messages...and then, after that initial week Tanner was away, there was only silence for three long months.

At first, Damon was pissed, because he'd grown to expect them, begun to hang on to every single one he received. But he knew that Tanner had to cut off all comms for his own good. It meant he was in a dangerous place doing dangerous things.

Tanner's fine.

And he kept telling himself that a hundred times a day, when he and LC worked on closing the sale of Crave and finding a new building to live in with lofts on the same floor. Actually, they decided to buy the building, keep the top floor for themselves and rent out the rest.

No more clubs, not for a while. But Crave was still his for another couple of months, and he had plans for Tanner and Room Four when the man returned.

He had to come back before the closing. Had to.

And still, there was nothing on the computer when he checked for the millionth time today, the same way there'd been nothing yesterday and the day before. Frustrated, Damon turned the computer off and pushed his chair back.

It was only then he realized he wasn't alone.

"You little fuck."

Tanner smiled from the corner. "I wanted to be able to surprise you, Damon. You can't take that away from me."

No, he couldn't. And as he stroked a hand through Tanner's hair and felt his steady, even heartbeat pressed against his chest, he knew that he was done worrying.

Mostly.

Epilogue

LC was sitting on the balcony of his new loft apartment—his had been renovated first, and he'd stayed at Damon's until it was finished. Now, Damon was staying with him. And things were quiet and calm, mainly because Tanner was away again with Delta.

Damon joined him, brining the whiskey and two glasses. LC took his neat and downed the first glass quickly.

"Guess we're getting drunk tonight," Damon said. "God, I miss that boy."

"Yeah, I do too." He'd grown quite close to Tanner.

"What about Paulo? Do you miss him?"

"It's only been a week since I talked to him."

"Three weeks, LC," Damon reminded him and LC winced. Paulo didn't deserve that shit from him. "What's going on? It's worse than usual."

"I talked to Styx."

Damon shot him a sharp glance across the table. "When?"

"After the attacks started. He actually picked up the phone." LC played with the glass of whiskey in front of him, remembered how Styx had called him Law—the only one to ever use that nickname on a regular basis—and he downed a double shot in a single gulp. His voice was huskier when he spoke again. "I told him I was done with him."

"Did you even ask him to come back first?"

LC shook his head. "I didn't want to know what his answer would be. If he'd wanted to come back to me, he would've by now. Same shit, different day."

"You've had ten years of that same day," Damon pointed out, although not unkindly.

"Nothing's going to change."

"And you're not going to let yourself move on."

LC didn't answer the question—not directly. "Styx came to the hospital."

"And?"

"He never let me know he was there." But LC knew, could feel Styx in the same way his bones told him when rain was coming.

He'd had so many broken by the time he was ten that there were days he ached more than an eighty-year-old, but he pushed himself through the pain. That kind of pain was easier to handle than the shit with Styx.

"You could've called to him," Damon pointed out.

"Yeah, but what would that change?"

"Maybe nothing. Maybe everything."

"Just don't fuck it up with Tanner, okay? One of us deserves a good relationship."

He hoped Damon wouldn't bring up Paulo. Paulo was handsome and good in bed but LC couldn't see past Styx, even ten years later.

He supposed that meant he never would.

"Both of us deserve it, Law," Damon said quietly, before leaving LC alone with his thoughts.

About the Author

SE Jakes lives in New York where she's currently at work penning her next book. She feels that doing what you love keeps you young and that writing about people falling in love is probably the best damned job in the entire world. You can find out more information about SE's newest books at sejakes.blogspot.com.

PUBLISHING

www.samhainpublishing.com

Green for the planet.
Great for your wallet.

It's all about the story...

Romance

HORROR

www.samhainpublishing.com

CPSIA information can be obtained
at www.ICGtesting.com
Printed in the USA
LVOW12s1020070916
503581LV00001B/69/P